When Private Breckles Enlisted

By

Donald Sinclair

authorHOUSE

AuthorHouse™
1663 Liberty Drive
Bloomington, IN 47403
www.authorhouse.com
Phone: 1 (800) 839-8640

Published by AuthorHouse 01/20/2016

ISBN: 978-1-5049-7237-6 (sc)
ISBN: 978-1-5049-7236-9 (e)

Library of Congress Control Number: 2016900255

Print information available on the last page.

Any people depicted in stock imagery provided by Thinkstock are models, and such images are being used for illustrative purposes only. Certain stock imagery © Thinkstock.

This book is printed on acid-free paper.

CHAPTER 1

Carl Breckles saw how the circle of land held by American troops around Pusan, Korea in 1950 was growing smaller. It was shoved on a small map there on the front page of the <u>Detroit News</u> he was folding for delivery. The "Perimeter," the news story called it, was down at the southern tip of Korea, at the port of Pusan, on the South China Sea, just across from Japan.

The concern was that invading North Koreans would push the Americans fighting along side the South Korean Army into the sea before more troops' supplies could be sent to the port.

Carl was sitting on the edge of the concrete slab outside the newspaper station, folding his newspapers, putting them in the bag, so he could put the bag in the basket on the front of his bike so they would be handy to sling on the porches as he rode along on his paper route.

Carl would be eighteen in two months, and was required by law to register with the draft board on his eighteenth birthday; and every copy of the newspaper he picked up had the small map on the front page, making him more concerned he might be sent to the war in Korea.

He, and everybody else of draft age did not like the mandatory two-years of military service, but remembering a television speech he heard by General Eisenhower that said it "was better to carry an eighty-pound pack -- than to wear Communist chains," he shook his head while stuffing the last folded newspaper into the bag.

Hefting the bag up into the bike basket, he said to himself, "Wonder if General Eisenhower ever carried an eighty pound pack on <u>his</u> back?

"I doubt it," he said, stopping a moment to watch a fight between two delivery guys, who had come late to the paper station, and one of them was going to be short fifteen copies because the truck delivery had been miscounted.

The paper station was nothing more than a garage with a light bulb, with board benches along the walls for the carriers to fold their newspapers on.

Carl moved his bike out of the way when the two guys started fighting, punching at one another's face, spilling out the open garage-wide doorway into the alley. The other paperboys were cheering them on -- smiling.

The station manager, a guy about nineteen, came to the doorway, a yellow pencil behind his ear, shouting for them to stop. He was worried; women in the houses nearby were constantly complaining to the Newspaper about the noise and swearing that frightened the kids in the backyards.

Carl, holding his bike handlebars, shouted at the station manager, "It's all your fault -- you should have ordered a few extra copies for the truck delivery. The News can afford it."

"Who asked you -- Breckles?"

"Somebody's got to tell you," Carl said pushing off on his bicycle, adding, "because you're a moron."

In the following months, Carl read on the newspaper front page, how General McArthur brought an army from Japan and launched an invasion from the sea at Inchon that cut the Korean peninsula in half.

Then he read later, how the Chinese "volunteers" spilled over the Yalu River into Korea in the north, to help their Korean "comrades" and were attacking McArthur's forces in "human waves."

The newspaper reported the fighting had turned into a bloodbath; the killing so extensive, that the blood ran down the hillsides and made ponds in the low places.

Carl had registered for the draft, and after a physical, was given a classification of 1-A, and could be called any time soon.

Shaking his head, folding his newspapers, reading the reports of the fighting in Korea, he said to himself, "I can't get into that mess over there -- I've got to do something -- to stay away from Korea."

It was after President Truman fired General McArthur, who wanted to use the Atomic Bomb on the Chinese, the President saying he did not want to start "a World War III," that Carl heard about Student Deferment.

Students attending college were given a 2-S Draft Classification, and did not have to go into the armed serves as long as they were enrolled in classes -- matriculating.

"I'm going to college," he told his parents at dinner.

They both smiled, looking at him; they knew he was a poor student, barely graduating high school.

"How you going to pay the tuition?" his father asked, folding his thick hands and putting his elbows on the table.

"I'll get a part-time job," Carl said slowly. "If I can live here, I can drive downtown to the Wayne University campus -- I'll buy a car with the money I've saved -- and I'll sell my paper route."

"It's wonderful," his mother said smiling at her daughter Amy, sitting next to her at the table, "our Carl going to college."

The daughter, and eighth-grader, looked across at Carl, "And what are you going to study?"

"I'd like to do something on a newspaper," Carl said slowly. "Maybe do some reporting -- write news stories."

'Well," his father said, "as long as you chip-in on the food bills -- I guess it's okay if you want to live here." He looked across the table at his wife, who was nodding.

*   *   *   *   *

Sitting in front of the lady advisor at the desk in the Wayne Admissions Office, Carl felt embarrassed. She was reading his grade transcript from Denby High School, and he knew about the D-grades in Civics and Algebra. What was worse, he had not graduated with his class.

After Summer School that following term, he gained the one hour he was short, and given his High School diploma in the principal's office. His parents were disappointed he did not wear a cap and gown, but they were more let down than he was.

He often wondered, how that gym teacher, Mr. Clark, could deprive a kid from graduating by withholding the one-hour credit for that stupid gym class.

"What we can do," the lady advisor said, pulling up her coat around her shoulders, covering the tweed suit she was wearing, "is have you take a test. It lasts about eight or nine hours, and it covers all the subjects; math, English, and science. We have to know what you know."

Carl could feel the cold now in the sixth-floor office of the poorly heated building that had once been a hotel. The University was buying old buildings all around the campus to expand classroom capacity, he had heard.

Most of the students of the University attended night classes after work. It was called a "lunch-bucket college."

"What day is the test?" Carl asked quietly; he had a dread of any kind of test.

"Saturday," the woman said pulling up the corner of her coat collar. "We give the test to all people who don't have a high grade average from high school."

Carl watched as she closed his file on her desk, and folded her hands, as if to say he would have to prove he could handle college-level classes.

"Okay," Carl said. "If that's what it takes to get admitted, I'll be here this Saturday."

"It's the only way we can determine if you have an aptitude for college level learning.

"And there is a fee -- fifty-five dollars."

"Wow," Carl said shaking his head. Then added, while putting his hands on the edge of the desk, "Okay -- I'll get the money."

"It begins at eight in the morning over in the auditorium at State Hall. You pay the test fee at the door."

"Okay," Carl said getting up slowly, wondering where he could get fifty-five dollars.

*   *   *   *   *

Three weeks later, Carl received a post card saying he should report to the college Admissions Office for the results of the daylong test.

It was snowing the afternoon he was back at the desk in front of the lady advisor. She was wearing a coat with a fur collar now, buttoned up to the neck.

"What would you do," she asked looking down at the salmon-colored card she held in front of her, "if you did not attend college?"

"Ah," Carl said wanting to conger up some bizarre job, sensing he was about to be admitted, "I was thinking of going up to Alaska -- become a Bush pilot."

"That's about what I thought," she said, laying the card flat on the desk, still looking at it.

Carl, looking close at the card, could see two parallel lines down the center; there were places where graph-like lines peaked outside the two parallel lines, and he guessed that was where he must have scored better than what was required to do college level classwork.

"You are going to be admitted to the college on "Probation Status," the woman said while reaching into a side desk drawer to take out a form paper. "If you get a grade C or better, you will be fully admitted for the term that follows."

"That's great," Carl said glancing at the snow falling outside the window. "I'll do my best to get good grades."

"You will only be permitted to take three classes while on the probationary period," the woman said writing on the form.

Carl nodded, looking at the snow, wondering what those two peaks on the salmon card were that went way over the center parallel lines. It must have been the peaks that impressed her.

He guessed it must be for Literature -- because he liked to read stories, especially the short stories with tricky endings. The novels were interesting too, he thought; you learned a lot of things following how people solved their problems.

Riding down the elevator in the Prentis Hall building from the Admissions Office, an old hotel Wayne State purchased and converted all the rooms to office, Carl was overcome with the feeling it was not much like a college, compared to the leafy campus he had seen in Ann Arbor when visiting his high school friends attending there.

Ann Arbor was going to a <u>real</u> college, he thought. There were longhaired girls dressed in pleated skirts, and students riding expensive English bicycles with skinny tires, and golden leaves covering the streets.

Wayne University was built around the old Central Detroit High School building at the corner of Cass and Warren Avenues. It was now called "Old Main."

The wood floors creaked when you walked in Old Main that was built at the turn of the century.

The college was expanding itself, buying abandon buildings in the campus neighborhood, some large houses that had been owned by families who made fortunes in lumber, politics and land speculation after the Civil War.

The Law School occupied a giant gray brick building that was low, like a ranch house. It was up Cass Avenue, north of Prentis Hall. The Theatre Arts building in Hillberry Auditorium was located up Woodward Avenue toward town, and the Medical School was at Harper Hospital a way further up Woodward. In the downtown city buildings, the Mortuary Science classes were held in the Detroit Coroner's Office near City Hall.

Carl found out during the winter days that many of the old residences had heating problems. But the worst came in the spring, when the ceiling of the residence his History class was being held in began leaking during a violent rainstorm. The class had to be cancelled.

Later, when he took night classes, he found most of the students had worked all day, some still wearing the wrinkled suits they had worn at the office earlier that day.

It was plain to see why Wayne State was labeled a "lunch bucket college." Most of the students were trying to better their station in life -- through education for their jobs and promotion. Carl understood all this -- he was one of them -- born in the Great Depression years like them.

None of these deficiencies were troublesome to Carl. He was content because the college was keeping him out of the Army and the Korean conflict.

* * * * *

That following summer, Carl, pressed for money, took a job on the assembly line at the Dodge Truck plant to earn the one hundred and twenty dollars for tuition in the coming Fall Term -- where he would begin his third full-time term -- fully matriculated because of his high grades.

The newspapers now began to report the Korean War was ebbing; a cease-fire was coming closer as both sides talked at Panmunjom. Despite a cease-fire being discussed, the shooting continued, and Carl meanwhile found out from another student, that he was eligible for the Army Draft until the age of twenty-six.

That would mean, Carl realized, even after graduating from college, he could still be drafted.

Sometimes, his college classes, which required a lot of study time, grew monotonous, almost like the repetition of installing the wing-windows on the doors of the truck cabs coming down the assembly line.

He did not know what he wanted, but he felt he needed to change his life; he thought about it all summer on the assembly line.

On a Saturday afternoon, at the end of the summer, the shadows growing longer, Carl decided to confront his father about leaving the grind he had been in for almost two years.

"I'm thinking of doing some travelling," he said to his father, polishing his light-green Chevrolet in the garage, the aluminum door open, up overhead. "Go away for a while."

"You mean you're going to quit the truck factory?" his father asked, shaking the polishing rag, then taking a drink of beer from the bottle on the workbench. There were two empty beer bottles at the end of the bench, next to the old refrigerator.

"I want to get away," Carl said folding his arms. "Go up north, Ishpeming -- or maybe take a drive out to Montana."

"Kid," his father said, setting the beer bottle on the bench, "when you got a steady job like you got -- with good pay -- you just don't throw it away. You find a nice girl -- and settle down -- buy a house."

"You got it wrong, dad," Carl said unfolding his arms. "The auto company can only let students work for the summer -- sixty days -- then the Union requires they have to join -- or you're out -- it's a union shop.

"If there is an opening, and you get hired, you end up on the night shift -- because you're at the bottom of the totem pole -- when it comes to seniority."

"But son, you got to hold on to a job -- when you get one -- out there. You just all of a sudden -- can't go quitting."

Carl watched his father roll up the sleeve of the faded flannel shirt that had dropped unfolded when he made a swinging gesture about quitting.

All of a sudden, Carl felt the need to get away even stronger now.

"Factory work is monotonous," Carl said leaning against the door jam. "It's doing the same thing -- every hour -- every day. I'm glad the summer's over -- and I'm out of the factory. I just want to get outside, Dad -- see things, places --"

"That's a bum's life, son," his father said, beginning to polish the car trunk lid. "You got to learn not to quit a job just because it's <u>monotonous</u>.

"Not until you got some other job lined up -- that you can go to."

"I was just earning money for college," Carl said, quietly. "That's why I went into that damn factory."

"Yeah," his father said turning to look at Carl, shaking the dust from the dry polish out of the rag. "You seem to be in that college a hell of a long time. How much longer you going to be stuck in there?"

"I'm almost at the one-third point," Carl said, "for the credits I need to graduate -- get a degree."

"Seems like you've been tied-up at that college an awfully long time, son," his father said, polishing again.

"I haven't said nothing about it -- you're mother asked me not to. But it seems to be taking more time than I thought."

"I know what you mean, Dad. It's been a strain on me too."

"I mean," his father said polishing down to the panel above the rear bumper, "you spend hours penned up in your bedroom --"

"I'm studying, Dad. It takes a lot of time to do all the reading for my classes."

"I've offered you a job with me," his father said, turning to look at Carl, "and time after time -- you say no.

"I'll teach you the ropes for handling heavy equipment -- bulldozer -- grader -- and you can get a job anywhere there's construction."

"I know," Carl said standing up straight from leaning. "I know -- and you are right, but I just don't want to be a heavy equipment operator, Dad. I'm sorry."

"It's your life, kid," his father said polishing down the right rear fender. "I'm just trying to help -- get you started in the right direction."

*   *   *   *   *

The day class registration for the Fall Term began, Carl went to the Admission Program, set up on tables in the Gymnasium at the Old Main Building.

He brought his checkbook in his shirt pocket to pay the tuition cost at the last table. You paid after you selected your classes and were given a punch card for each class.

The old varnished wood floor of the gym was covered with a heavy dark-green canvas to keep it from being scuffed. Sometimes people stumbled, tripped by a fold of canvas that rose up from the floor.

Carl was putting his checkbook back in his shirt pocket after paying the tuition, and going through the double door of the gym, out into the hallway, saw the sign over the military recruiter's table:

TOUR EUROPE WHILE YOU SERVE YOUR COUNTRY

"How can you be sure you'll be sent to Europe?" Carl asked the middle-aged Sergeant at the desk. He wore the wool olive-drab uniform of World War II, and the short jacket called an "Eisenhower" that only came to the hips.

The Sergeant smiled up at Carl.

"The Army is activating a new Division at Fort Riley, Kansas," he said in a business-like tone. "When it's trained, it will be shipped to Germany -- Wurzburg -- to replace the First Division -- that's been there since the end of the war."

"That's going to take a lot of time," Carl said. "I mean filling up a Division -- your two year tour will be over before you get there to Wurzburg."

"No Draftees," the Sergeant said leaning back in his chair, all the strips of his medals showing over his left pocket. "You have to enlist for three years -- you have to have at least two years left in your enlistment -- or they don't ship you over there.

"It will take a year to fill up the three regiments in the new Division -- and train them at Fort Riley. Then when the First Division is shipped to Fort Riley -- you serve two years in Germany -- the Occupation Forces -- in their place over there.

"The Army calls it Operation Switchback."

"But it means," Carl said, "you have to sign up for an extra year in the Army."

"That's right," the Sergeant said leaning forward onto the table, looking up at Carl. "A Draftee only serves two years -- they can't join the operation."

"Let me think it over," Carl said.

That evening at supper, Carl, watching his mother set a long casserole dish of sauerkraut with baked sausage at the center of the table, said "I decided I'm not going back to the University this fall. I want to take some time off -- and travel."

"Didn't you register?" his father asked sitting down.

"I did," Carl said. "But I went back and cancelled the classes, and got a tuition refund. They didn't like it."

"What about the Army," his sister asked. "Won't they draft you now -- if you're not in college?"

"I'm going in the Army," Carl said quietly. "In about a year -- after training -- I'll go to Europe for two years -- guaranteed. That's the special program I signed up for."

"Where?" his father asked scooping sauerkraut on his plate. "Where in Europe?"

"Germany," Carl said softly.

"Oh my goodness," his mother said, and sat down.

CHAPTER 2

The third Sunday morning at Fort Riley, the recruits were allowed to sleep in until breakfast. There was no reveille.

Carl was lying on his unmade bunk, writing a quick letter home on a tablet from the PX. There was not much time to write during the week; they went from one training session -- a Military Courtesy lecture, or to a lesson on how to disassemble an M-1 rifle and its nomenclature, in a steady flow of information classes that occupied most of the day. The day began at 5 am.

The recruits, after morning Physical Training exercises, were constantly marching to some distant training hall. But, within another few weeks, the Company would be up to full strength of a hundred and fifty men, they were told, and Basic Infantry Training would begin in earnest. Until that time, the recruits were given the training classes.

"You got anything you need washed?" Carl heard someone ask, and looked up to see a soldier with a white nametag reading LASSLETT, standing at the end of his bunk. "Shirts or socks -- I'll wash them for a quarter."

Carl had seen him talking to recruits up and down the rows of bunks, several days now, but he never knew what he was talking about.

"No," Carl said, looking back at his writing pad letter, "I washed out my stuff last night."

When Lasslett turned away, Carl took a quick look at him again. He looked unusually thin, his fatigues hanging loosely, the appearance of someone who had missed meals, been deprived of food, for some time.

Carl thought he must have joined the army to survive in life -- maybe because he could not find work.

In the PX cafeteria two nights later, Carl sat at a table reading a thick paperback novel, "From Here to Eternity," he had just bought. He had three dollars left until payday, two days away, so he bought only a cup of coffee.

Lasslett came up to the table, carrying a bottle of Hamm's beer sold in the cafeteria.

"Mind if I sit here?"

Carl looked up and shook his head.

"That's a thick book," Lasslett said sitting down, setting the beer bottle in front of him on the table, but still holding it.

"It's about Army life in Hawaii just before Pearl Harbor," Carl said lifting the book to look at the cover. "They're going to make a movie, I hear.

"I bought it to pass the time to payday, keep me from thinking about money."

"Payday," Lasslett said, sitting up straight, taking a drink of beer, quickly. "I need money so bad it hurts. I send everything I can -- back to my wife in Wisconsin -- all but a few bucks for myself.

"She just had a baby," he said shifting his weight in the chair, adjusted, "and it's been rough."

Carl realized Lasslett was a bit older than most of the recruits, and now he was aware there was a reason for his joining the Army; but he just nodded.

"How come they always make you Barracks Orderly?" Carl asked, folding the corner of the page in the book to mark where he had stopped reading.

He knew Lasslett did not attend the lectures the other recruits did.

"Prior service," Lasslett said slowly lifting the beer bottle, hesitating. "I was in the Air Force -- Korea. I've been through the classes like Military Courtesy and that stuff before."

"The First Sergeant knows that, huh?" Carl asked, sliding the novel forward on the table, listening.

"Yeah, he does," Lasslett said, draining what beer was left in the bottle.

"When I was discharged from the Air Force and came home, I got married. But jobs were few and far between -- then I lost my truck.

"So with the baby -- I decided to go back in the Air Force, but they were full-up -- so I joined the Army -- for the steady money."

"And now you scuffle around the barracks for quarters, doing other people's dirty laundry -- to earn walk-around money," Carl said, in a tone that was not insulting, but understanding.

"That's about the size of it," Lasslett said. Then, holding up the empty bottle, added, "I'm going to get another brew."

Smiling, Carl said, "That beer is only three-point-two alcohol. I heard about it in college -- Hamm's makes it in Ohio so the kids on campus there can't get too swacked on it. It's half the alcohol of regular beer."

"It's all I can get," Lasslett said getting up from his chair, "and -- it's better than nothing," he said and walked away to the cafeteria counter.

Carl finished his coffee, then got up, sliding the paperback book off the table, then walked toward the exit door and said to himself, "Wonder what he would say -- if I told him I joined the Army to travel?"

The next evening in the barracks, when Lasslett came asking around for washing, Carl gave him a pair of socks and paid him a quarter.

After supper on payday, Carl walked over to the PX where most of the recruits had made a run for.

Opening the door, he stepped into where the long line at the cigarette counter ended just inside the front entrance. He dodged a second line where guys were holding new socks and t-shirts, others shaving cream cans, razors and toothbrushes, the things needed for the coming weeks; Basic Training was scheduled to start next Monday.

After buying one of the low alcohol beers, Carl turned to the cafeteria, and spotted Lasslett sitting at a table in the corner. He was writing in a tablet, a beer bottle on the table.

"Catching up on writing home?" Carl said sitting down in the chair opposite him.

"Yeah, my wife wants to come here," he said looking at Carl, making a grimace, dropping the pen. "She wants to be here with me -- she and the baby. She says she's -- lonely -- there back in Wisconsin."

Carl took a quick sip of beer; "The Army don't want recruit's wives here -- besides we're going to be shipping overseas right after training."

"I ain't going to tell them she's here," he said raising his beer bottle slowly.

Carl, smiling, shrugged.

He watched as Lasslett took a money order out of his fatigue jacket pocket, tear off the stub, and fold it inside the pages of the letter.

"They won't give you a pass every night to go home, when she comes," Carl said watching Lasslett seal the envelope, then begin writing the address on the front. "you know that."

"Maybe on weekends," Carl said leaning back in his chair, looking away from Lasslett, "if you're lucky. But only <u>after</u> Basic Training is over."

"We'll have to work something out," Lasslett said. "I've written her, and we can get a place over in Junction City -- a trailer maybe -- something not too expensive."

He stood up.

"I'm going to mail this letter right now," he said waiving the letter as if it were hot.

Carl looked away, and taking out a dollar bill from his jacket, handed it to Lasslett.

"Get four beers over there," he said, "if they'll let you have that many at one time."

"You bet."

Carl watched as Lasslett mailed the letter in the box next to the cashier counter, then move over to the cooler for the beer.

"He just put his head in a noose," he said quietly, sipping beer. "The Army is going to come down on him like a ton of bricks.

"He knows that -- he's been in the service before. They can make life miserable -- if they want to."

When Lasslett came back to the table with four bottles of beer, he said, "Let's have a celebration -- I feel like celebrating my wife Jackie's coming here."

"Me," Carl said as Lasslett sat down at the table, "I'm just glad we're finally going to start Basic Training. I've had enough of this Pre-Cycle Training crap all these weeks."

"Right," Lasslett said, sliding two bottles across the table to Carl, "you can celebrate Basic -- and I'll drink to seeing my family again."

"That sounds reasonable," Carl said. "We'll be just like the soldiers in the "From Here to Eternity" book I'm reading. They go to some club in Honolulu for booze and girls."

"We're here in Kansas," Lasslett said, lifting a bottle of beer, "where the Geographical Center of the United States -- is around here someplace nearby. There's a monument. We're a long way from Honolulu -- man."

"In that case," Carl said, "the only thing to do -- is drink a lot of beer -- for the -- deficiency."

"I should have thought of that," Lasslett said.

"Say," Carl said suddenly, "what the hell is your first name?" Carl asked when Lasslett came back to the table the third time.

"Mike," Lasslett blurted while sitting down.

"Michael Lasslett," Carl said, slowly. "Sounds like the name of a -- piano player -- something like that."

"No -- I had a small business putting in fence posts. But -- I lost it. Maybe I should have went to college, like you, and learned to play the piano -- and I wouldn't be here."

At five minutes to eight, the civilian clerk, who worked in the PX cafeteria, came over to the table wiping his hands in his apron.

"Closing time," he said calmly. "We are required to close down the store -- promptly at eight every night."

"Is it <u>that</u> late -- already?" Carl said.

The clerk began to collect the twelve empty beer bottles on the table. He was a gray-haired man who took his work seriously.

"We don't usually let customers have this many beers," he said. "Not at one time."

"Tonight was a special celebration," Lasslett said. "We have a lot to celebrate -- don't we Carl?"

"Yep," Carl said, before lifting the last bottle to drain it, "we had to double-celebrate -- on half strength beer."

"You boys are a little woozy," the clerk said, "but you still have to be off the premises at eight o'clock prompt.

Lasslett stood up slowly, leaning to his left, unsteady.

"Yessir," he said, pulling his Eisenhower jacket down on his hips. "Your orders -- are my command."

Carl stood up, both hands on the table, feeling the effect of the beer.

"Wish I had twelve more beers -- make a <u>real</u> party."

"You guys better get going," the clerk said, "the CQ officer will be making his rounds any minute in his Jeep. You could get us in a jam -- for giving you all this beer."

"We're going," Lasslett said leading the way to the door. They were the last soldiers to leave.

Outside, standing at the bottom of the wooden steps of the PX, Carl waved his arm, "Boy, I feel good. For the first time in weeks -- I'm not feeling down in the dumps. And I like it. I mean I don't want it to go away.

"No wonder the soldier in the "From Here to Eternity" book says 'It's a soldier's sacred duty -- to get drunk on payday,' or something like that."

"You know what, Carl," Lasslett said looking up at the overhead light on the front of the PX building, and the darkness all around, "it ain't very far from here to Junction City -- just over that hill is the roadway. We could have -- more beer -- a lot more."

"I'm tired of taking classes," Carl said. "I joined the army to get away from college classes. All I been doing in the army -- is going to classes."

"You got any money you can loan me, Carl?"

"I got my pay," Carl said, "except what the Company Commander made me put in that Soldier's Deposits Saving Fund."

"Let's go in to Junction City," Lasslett said looking out into the dark. "We'll come back by eleven -- make bed check."

CHAPTER 3

They walked quickly up the grassy ridge behind the PX building, then started down the steep slope to the roadway that ran alongside the Army camp.

It was dark now, out of the lights, and Carl fell to his knees.

"Hey," he laughed, "that three-two beer hit me like a brick -- I'm kind of dizzy."

"Yeah," Lasslett said, stopping to pull him up, grabbing hold of the uniform cloth at the shoulder, "you drink enough of it -- it's just like regular beer."

"Well then," Carl waved his arm to get the cloth of his jacket back in place, "I can claim I was drunk -- when they throw me in the Stockade -- for going AWOL."

"Naw," Lasslett said as Carl was brushing the knees of his uniform pants, "you're just a trainee -- they won't throw you in the clink. They'll just give you Company punishment -- KP for a week straight -- something like that."

"What do they expect?" Carl said standing up straight, indignantly, "I've been in the Army six weeks -- and no Basic Training yet -- and no passes to town either."

"You got that right," Lasslett said as they were walking along the edge of the road. "Most recruits would be done with Basic by this time."

"Yeah, it's a pain in the ass," Carl said looking at the lights up ahead where Junction City began, "all the waiting -- while they fill up the Regiment with bodies."

"Hope we can find a bar," Lasslett said as they walked, "or maybe a liquor store -- get a few more beers. Make this trip worthwhile."

"I sure could use a beer," Carl said. "Hey what's that over there?"

Up the road, on the opposite side, was a dark building with a neon sign glowing red: SUGAR SHACK.

"I think this is the Colored part of town," Lasslett said quietly.

"Well," Carl said, "I ain't prejudice -- if they got cold beer."

"I hope they ain't either," Lasslett said laughing.

As they walked closer, they saw a row of cottages alongside the bar building; the view from the road had been blocked by a giant Weeping Willow tree that stood at the edge of the road.

A thin woman stepped out of the shadow of the tree trunk.

"You boys looking for a good time?" she said smiling. "I hear you guys got paid over there in the camp. You looking for a girl?"

"My wife's coming next week," Lasslett said.

Carl, looking at the short leopard jacket she wore, the small purse hanging on the chain over her shoulder, and her thin legs, grew excited.

"How much is a good time?" he asked.

"I'm Hildy -- from Kansas City -- I get five bucks."

"You the only girl here?" Lasslett asked.

"I'm the only white one honey."

Carl was reaching into his pocket, looking for money. He counted out five single bills.

"Okay," Lasslett said stepping away, "you two enjoy yourself. I'm going over to the bar."

"I got six weeks to make up for," Carl said putting his arm around the girl's shoulders as they started toward the cabins. He put his face against the girl's.

"Mine is the second one," Hildy said as she took the money from his hand. "The second cabin from the end."

She turned on the light in the wood floor cabin when they entered. There was a narrow metal bed, a table and a dresser painted white next to the bed.

She took off her leopard jacket and set it next to the purse on the dresser.

"Just drop your pants, honey," she said, pulling up her dress and sitting on the edge of the bed. She wore nothing underneath. "I'm going to have a busy night -- tonight. It's payday."

"Oh man," Carl said sliding down his pants, sitting next to her on the bed, "you look terrific --"

"No, no," Hildy said, "we don't have time to do the high school stuff, honey."

She lay back on the bed and opened her legs.

"I'm going to explode," Carl said pressing down on her. "You -- look great -- babe. It's been too long --"

"That's it, honey," Hildy said. "That's -- it -- that's," Hildy whispered, as Carl thrusted, she was thrusting back, "my soldier."

When Carl climaxed, she pushed him off her, and slid off the bed, and holding up her dress, was wiping herself.

"Let's do it again, Hildy," Carl said still lying on the bed.

"Not tonight, honey," she said dropping her dress. "It's payday. Hildy will have a lot of customers tonight. Up soldier," she said swinging her leopard jacket over her shoulder, "pull your pants up. Time to go."

"I can pay," Carl said, standing, pulling on his uniform pants. "Let's do it again -- babe."

"I got regular customers honey," Hildy said opening the door. "They come to the bar -- for me -- I'm a big attraction -- around here. Some other time -- we'll get together, soldier," she said, hitting him lightly in the crotch, as he was putting on his uniform hat.

Walking toward the bar in the dark, Carl kissed her hard.

"No more now," she said pushing him away. "This is strictly business. Go up to the bar," she said stepping back. "Boy, you must have been in that camp a long time -- too long."

Carl watched as she moved away in the dark, then turned, walking slowly up to the bar doorway.

As Carl came up to the front of the bar that had been a farmhouse, two Negro Sergeants stepped out. They looked at Carl, but said nothing as they went to their car.

When Carl pulled open the bar door, a burst of Dixieland music hit him in the face. He stood looking around the room, until he saw Lasslett sitting at the end of the bar.

"How'd it go?" Lasslett asked smiling.

"It left me -- wanting -- more," Carl said sitting down on the stool next to him.

When the bartender came over, a short Negro with a round face wearing a white shirt, Carl said, "I'll have a Budweiser."

"This is a restaurant," the bartender said smiling.

Carl looked at Lasslett, who was smiling widely.

"Those are all whiskey bottles on the shelf back there," Carl said defensively.

"Them's all bought," the bartender said calmly reaching for two bottles. "They got the buyer's names -- see."

Carl could read the two names: "Jones" on one, "Beaumont" on the other, printed on a white piece of tape.

He realized he was being kidded.

"What's the catch?" he said pointing at the Budweiser bottle on the bar in front of Lasslett.

"There're no bars in Kansas -- you got to buy the whiskey and beer from the liquor store up front," Lasslett said grinning.

"Yeah," the bartender said setting the two bottles back on the display behind the bar, "we can only sell the mixes -- and the ice with the glasses. And we can keep the bottle of whiskey here -- for when you come next time."

Carl, grinning, leaning back on his stool, caught a glimpse of other customers watching.

"I get it," he said, noticing that suddenly the customers seemed relieved that he understood the bar practices.

"I can buy a bottle then," Carl said putting his hand in his wool uniform pocket, feeling the twenty and ten dollar bills he had carefully folded.

"I got to get it from the store up front," the bartender said, both hands resting on the bar in front of him, waiting for the order.

"Bourbon," Carl said.

"A quart?" the bartender asked quietly.

"No, a pint," Carl said.

Carl watched the bartender take a ring of keys from under the bar, then walk to the door at the far end and unlock a door with a metal grille over the glass, and go through.

"How come they have this crazy set-up in the bars here in Kansas?" Carl asked Lasslett.

"It started at the beginning of the century," Lasslett said. "You've heard of Carrie Nation, the crazy old dame who used to go in bars with an axe and smash the whiskey bottles. That was over here in Wichita."

"Didn't nobody stop her?"

"Naw," Lasslett said taking a drink of his Budweiser, "the women were all behind it -- I think it lead to Prohibition -- when the women got the vote. The women were for her."

When the bartender came back, he said, "Old Crow okay?"

"Yeah," Carl said, taking out his carefully folded bills, sliding out the ten and setting it on the counter.

"Three dollars," the bartender said, running his hand over the shoulder of the pint bottle wiping the dust away.

While the bartender turned to ring up the sale on the cash register, Carl said, "I'll trade you a shot of Old Crow for some of your Budweiser."

"Have a can," Lasslett said. "I bought a six-pack -- ask the bartender for one."

"I thought you were broke," Carl said pealing the plastic off the top of the bottle.

"I got seventy cents left," Lasslett said, watching the bartender count the change on the bar.

"You want a mix for your drink?" he said looking down the bar where a customer raised his hand for a refill.

"No," Carl said. "Just two shot glasses."

As the bartender moved away, a heavy negro woman in a bright yellow dress stepped behind Carl's barstool, "You boys looking for a good time?"

"No thanks," Carl said scooping the money off the bar, "we're going to be leaving."

When the woman moved away, Carl was saying, "I'd like to go with Hildy again," just as the bartender brought two shot glasses.

"We don't let that Hildegard in here no more," he said. "She's sick."

"You mean I'm going to get -- the clap?" Carl asked.

"Not sex-sick," the bartender said. "Some of the other girls told me when she coughs -- blood comes up. So I told her I don't need none of that -- here in the bar. I told her to keep out of here."

Lasslett, laughing at Carl, downed the bourbon from the shot glass.

"Sounds like TB, Carl," Lasslett said. "Have a shot of bourbon -- and hope it kills the germs."

Carl drank a quick shot, and after pouring another in his glass, then filled Lasslett's glass, thinking.

"Maybe she's just got an ulcer -- or something like that," Carl said.

Picking up his shot glass, Lasslett said, "Let's hope so, kid."

Half the pint bottle was gone, and they had finished Lasslett's six-pack, when, leaning against the bar with his elbow, he said, "I want to see my wife. I got to see Jacqueline."

"Yeah," Carl said looking at Lasslett; seeing he was growing maudlin, not knowing what to say.

"I lost my job," Lasslett said looking at Carl, "then I lost my pick-up truck -- and now -- I'm going to lose Jackie."

"You better lay off the Old Crow," Carl said slowly.

"I'm going home," Lasslett said, sliding heavily off the barstool, holding the edge of the bar.

"Everything okay down here?" the bartender asked in a concerned voice as he came down the bar.

"We figure it's time to go," Carl said screwing on the cap to the pint. "We've had enough to hold us for a while," he said getting to his feet, then, taking out his money, set a dollar on the bar.

"You put away a lot of that bottle fast," the bartender said scooping up the bill. "You gonna be all right?"

"The air will do us good," Carl said following Lasslett to the door.

"Watch out for the MPs," was the last Carl heard him say before the door slammed.

They were walking along the roadway, out of the lights of the roadhouse, when Lasslett said, "It ain't right -- I mean, me losing everything. Don't somebody owe me something? I fought for this country in Korea -- and I end up with nothing."

"You were in -- Korea?" Carl asked, surprised.

"I was a 'kicker'" Lasslett said "on a Dakota -- a DC3 -- I did a lot of loading and unloading -- and when we did parachute drops -- I kicked the stuff out the door."

"You win any medals?" Carl stopped, taking out the pint from his hip pocket, drinking.

Lasslett stopped walking, and taking the bottle said, "Naw. One time we had to leave an airstrip -- in a hurry -- when the Gooks showed up unexpected, while they were turning the plane around."

"We didn't know the outpost was overrun," Lasslett said taking a drink. "I used a BAR to keep them off the airstrip, and we got off. The Captain said he was putting me in for a medal -- but I never got it," he said handing the bottle back to Carl.

"That's tough luck," Carl said holding up the pint to check the amount left. "We better take it easy on the booze -- this has got to last."

"We'll get more," Lasslett said in a loud voice, and Carl knew the whiskey was hitting him hard. "We'll get some bourbon in Topeka."

"Topeka?" Carl said, as they walked. "You crazy? How we going to get to Topeka?"

"Hitchhike," Lasslett said calmly, walking. "We're in uniform -- and people like to give soldiers a ride. They feel they owe soldiers something, I guess."

"Hitchhike," Carl said grinning, "you must be crazy."

"I might hitchhike all the way to Wisconsin -- La Crosse," Lasslett said. "I want to see Jackie and the baby."

"You better lay off the Old Crow," Carl said. "You're beginning to go off the deep end -- you're throwing a wet blanket over our party. You're getting too -- serious."

Car headlights showed in the dark distance of the road behind them.

"Stick your thumb out," Lasslett said, and turning a round stumbled. "We got our ride to Topeka -- coming."

"You're sick in the head," Carl said, sliding his hands in his pockets, watching as Lasslett raised his arm up, the thumb extended.

When the car stopped next to them, Carl saw it was painted olive drab; a four-door Chevy with numbers stenciled on the hood.

"Ah -- shit," Carl said quietly. "Forget Topeka -- we're going to the Stockade. We'll be doing the 'Stockade-shuffle.'"

All soldiers knew the "Shuffle," where a step forward was taken with one leg, and the other leg dragged up to it -- as if the weight of a ball-and-chain were dragged as a prisoner walked.

Officers prohibited the "Shuffle" on the Fort Riley grounds; it was considered a protest against the army discipline, and sign of contempt.

Riding inside the dark car, Carl said to the driver, "Is this an Army car?" knowing full well that it was.

"Yes," the driver said. "You guys on pass?"

"Nah," Lasslett said, "we're just out for a walk."

Suddenly, the driver half-turned in the front seat, and holding out a Forty-five Automatic at Carl, said, "you men are under arrest. I'm with the CID Division of the Military Police."

"What took you so long?" Lasslett said, grinning.

"Put that thing down," Carl said, growing sober quickly. "We're not criminals."

The driver picked up a radio microphone from the car dashboard, after he lowered the gun.

"Yes, base," he said, "this is car twenty-one, Sergeant Caldwell. I'm bringing in two suspects -- possible AWOL -- call the OD at the Guard House. They look like Trainees -- no Infantry badge on their lapels -- only two US brass badges.

"Right. I'll be at headquarters in about fifteen minutes," the Sergeant said and hung the microphone back on the dashboard.

Lasslett leaned toward Carl, "We'll probably face a firing-squad in the morning."

"Knock off the comedy," Carl said.

"I demand to call my lawyer," Lasslett said, nodding.

At the headquarters Guard House, they were told to sit on the bench in the lobby.

"What Regiment you from?" Sergeant Caldwell asked, while writing on a clipboard.

"Fifty-fifth," Carl said. "Fox Company."

Another Sergeant at a table and holding a telephone, said to Caldwell, "The OD said to call their Company for a Jeep to come pick them up -- return them to barracks."

"I guess they ain't going to put us in the clink," Lasslett said grinning at Carl.

Riding in the back of the open Jeep, the two guys from the Company up front, Carl nudged Lasslett in the dark, showing that an inch of Old Crow remained in the pint.

Lasslett took a long drink; then Carl finished the bottle, turning his face sideways to hide his drinking, and dropped the empty over the side of the Jeep.

"Damn," Lasslett said, "I miss my wife," and lowered his head. "Hope she comes here -- when she gets my letter.

"Or -- I don't know what I'm going to do."

"Maybe," Carl said, "you should have banged that dame in the yellow dress -- when you had the chance -- you know -- to ease your mind."

"I don't have any money," Lasslett said. "But I doubt if it would have helped any."

Carl saw the two soldiers in the front of the Jeep look at one another; they were listening to the talk about women.

*   *   *   *   *

The following Saturday fourteen Trainees went AWOL to Junction City.

Word had spread quickly in the barracks that Carl and Lasslett were only given Company Punishment -- a week's KP that included cleaning the Mess Hall grease trap -- but they were not Court Martialed.

Because Carl could type, he was given the job of charting each soldier's record of training during Basic as it progressed. He spent most of the day in the Company Headquarters.

Lasslett was later assigned to take Basic Training with Item Company over in the Third Battalion.

The Army split-up the two trouble makers.

CHAPTER 4

Carl had come to the PX to buy a new box of envelopes, after he found the supply in his footlocker stuck closed.

He was sitting at a table in the cafeteria, addressing a letter home.

"Hey Carl," Lasslett said, "long time no see," walking up to the table and setting down a cup of coffee, but still holding a bag of potato chips.

Carl slipped the letter into the envelope, and smiling, licked the top flap quickly, and sealed it closed.

"See you survived Basic Training over there in Item Company," he said setting the envelope down.

"Yeah," Lasslett said ripping open the bag, then crunching a potato chip in his mouth, "it all worked out -- I get along over there with everybody -- I guess I'm sort of a celebrity."

"I'm in a hurry about taking Advance Unit Training -- get it out of the way -- settle down -- into the Army routine after."

Carl sat looking across the table, sensing Lasslett was holding back something, so he just nodded.

"My wife is here," Lasslett blurted, then crunching another chip, took a quick sip of coffee.

"What about the Army regulation no wives for enlisted men?" Carl asked slowly. "You know we're headed for Germany once we get through Advance Basic?"

"Too late now," Lasslett said pointing, "That's her at the counter over there -- buying the laundry soap and those rugs. She's been here for over a week -- with the baby -- we got a trailer rented in Junction City. She sold her Nash Rambler -- we got some cash ahead."

Most of the soldiers in the cafeteria were looking at her; she looked a double for Sandra Dee in her ponytail hairdo and Poodle skirt, like she had just stepped out of a movie with Frankie Avalon.

Somebody put a quarter in the cafeteria jukebox, and the record "Cherry Pink and Apple blossom White" began to play, the trumpet blaring.

Lasslett, smiling, stood up at the table as she was walking over carrying the things she had bought.

Carl caught her walk; he watched her thin legs rising, making the Poodle skirt flare-up almost like the prance of a show horse.

Her bouncing black ponytail added to the illusion.

To Carl, the blaring trumpet on the jukebox made the subtle impression he was watching a floorshow, and he grinned.

"Holy mackerel," he said, under his breath, watching Lasslett kiss the side of her face, then take the things she had bought in the commissary from her hands, and set them on a chair.

"Jackie," he said, "this is Carl Breckles."

Carl was nodding when he noticed her smile showed even teeth; she was well cared for, the princess of the family, he thought to himself.

He was wondering how a wanderer like Lasslett came to meet her, when she said, "Michael has told me about you," as she was sitting down, "in his letters -- the adventures you two were involved in."

"They weren't exactly 'adventures'" -- Carl said picking up his letter, smiling, "they were more like -- desperate endeavors."

Lasslett, grinning at her, said, "Have you got all the stuff you brought unpacked?"

He moved his chair closer to hers, and sat down.

"Almost," she said. "Hey, you know things are a lot cheaper here at the PX than the stores in Junction City," avoiding the question.

Carl realized then she still wore the better clothes people dress in for travelling; she was not much interested in unpacking.

She seemed more interested in viewing the surroundings.

Carl, shaking the letter, said, "I'm going to mail this -- be back in a second." As he leaned out of the chair to stand up, he caught a glimpse of Jackie's legs as she was crossing them just then, and there was the flash of a round thigh.

Near the mailbox, two soldiers dressed in fatigues were sitting at a table drinking beer.

"Whose those guys with the cheerleader over there at the table?" Carl heard one soldier ask the other.

Carl grinned, dropping his letter in the slot.

"They're the ones who went over the hill -- first," the other said, lifting his beer bottle. "The first guys in the Regiment to go AWOL."

"They seem buddy-buddy," the guy asking the question said, pressing his fatigue hat down just above his eyes.

"Wonder if all three of them -- share a bed too?"

Carl was walking past the two soldiers, back toward his table, when he heard the soldier with the beer bottle add, laughing, "Who knows -- you never can tell."

Carl felt the back of his neck flush hot; he never thought of what being a friend of Lasslett meant now. What it might look like to other people.

It was a joke, but it hit Carl hard, and he was not sure of what to do.

Sitting down at the table again, he heard Lasslett ask, "Tell me what you <u>really</u> think of the trailer?"

"Mom likes it because it's clean," she said indifferently looking around the cafeteria.

"It's roomy," he said, leaning back in his chair. "We were lucky to find a place -- at all."

"Ah -- so you found a trailer?" Carl asked.

"Yeah. We're in the Prairie View Park -- just outside of Junction City," Lasslett said, gloating at the find. "A Sergeant in Item Company told me about it -- he was transferring out to Fort Ord in California."

Carl watched Jackie open her leather purse on the table, take out a pack of Kool cigarettes, and light one. She seemed not much interested in the subject being talked about.

Carl sat thinking, here she was a new mother, but she did not act like one. She acted like a spoiled teenager.

"You want a Coke?" Lasslett asked her in a tone that said he wanted to do something for her. "Maybe a coffee?"

"No," she said, snubbing out the cigarette. "I just remembered -- I forgot shampoo. I'll go to the Commissary, get the shampoo and run back to the trailer. I've been gone too long already."

"Who's watching the baby?" Carl asked.

"My Step-mother is here with me," she said. "She came on the train with me and the baby -- to sort of help out in getting resettled."

When she stood up, lifting her purse, Lasslett said, "I'll come with you to the taxi."

"No-no," she said quickly, "but be sure to bring the shopping bags home when you get off duty."

"Okay," he said, sitting back down slowly, raising his eyebrows, instead of making a shrug.

Carl smiled, watching her cross the cafeteria floor in her prancing step, aware every eye was on her.

"You old dog," Carl said to Lasslett, "she really looks young."

When he leaned back in his chair, Carl heard someone say behind him, in a low voice, "How'd you like to chase that around the bedroom?"

"She was twenty," Lasslett said, intently watching her go into the Commissary section of the PX, distracted, "two months ago."

"How did you meet her?" Carl asked, after she disappeared behind a stock shelf.

"Her family owns a dairy farm," Lasslett said, taking a sip of his cold coffee. "They were building a fence across the barnyard -- and I was hauling posts and lumber -- a part time job for the lumber yard -- and I made four -- or five trips."

Carl, grinning, said, "So you met the farmer's daughter, heh?"

"Not until," Lasslett said grinning, "her father asked me to help dig post-holes," Lasslett said relaxing now from being tense.

"It was summer, hot, and we spent all day digging -- then one day, Jackie and her sister came around."

"And when you saw her," Carl said, "it was love at first sight?"

Smiling, Lasslett said, "Her older sister -- is a little on the heavy side," while lighting a cigarette.

The PX cafeteria attendant walked over to the next table from where they were sitting.

"We're closing in ten minutes," he said putting cups and plates on a tray he had carried over.

He was a short man, growing bald; Carl nodded looking at him. "Okay."

Then to Lasslett, he said, "This Saturday, the Army is giving the Company a twelve-hour pass -- noon to midnight. If you can get out," Carl said, "we usually drink at the Arrowhead Bar in Junction City. They got a pool table."

Lasslett shrugged, and said, "We'll see --" while leaning back in his chair. "I'm helping with cleaning the trailer -- when the Army let's me off - in the evening."

Carl watched as Lasslett picked up the two paper-shopping bags his wife had left on the chair.

"You two must be spending a fortune on taxi fares," Carl said.

"Nah," Lasslett said holding a bag in each arm, "it's only seventy-five cents to the trailer park from camp -- wish I had my truck though -- it would make things easier."

They were walking to the door of the PX.

"How'd you lose the truck?" Carl asked, as he moved a chair out of their way.

"We were just married," Lasslett said, "living in town at La Crosse -- when a guy I served with in Korea showed up. We did a lot of talking and drinking one night -- and driving home, I got stopped by a State Trooper."

Carl laughed, pushing the bar to open the heavy exit door.

"Yeah," Lasslett said going through the doorway, "it was my third drunk-driving arrest -- and I got ninety days."

"But how'd you lose the truck?"

"I didn't make the payments on it the three months I was in jail."

"So there went your pick-up," Carl said, grinning.

"And Jackie was pregnant," Lasslett said quietly as they walked to the taxi parked across the street, under the overhead lights, "so I needed a regular payday -- fast.

"Like I told you, the Air Force recruiter was full-up, so I went over to the Army -- and here I am."

"It worked out okay," Carl said opening the taxi door.

Sitting down in the back of the taxi, still holding the two shopping bags, Lasslett said, "I forgot to tell you -- I heard through the grapevine -- I'm going to be sent back to Fox Company."

"How come?" Carl said grinning. "They always transfer out the Black Sheep."

"The Company lost five or six guys, who requested Officer's Candidate School in Georgia -- Fort Benning. They're gone. The Company is under strength, so they sent for me."

Shaking his head, Carl slammed the taxi door, not saying anything.

Watching the taxi drive away, Carl thought a moment, and said, "I hope Fox Company knows what it's doing -- transferring him back."

At first, as he was walking back to the barracks, he thought of Lasslett serving ninety-days in jail, then the question popped into his mind:

"What was Jackie doing -- while he was in the clink?"

*   *   *   *   *

The time of living in a tent during the weeks of Advance Basic went by quickly. The only excitement came when a Kansas windstorm blew down the canvas shelters.

The officers were telling everybody the storm made the training more realistic, but no one was impressed, as they looked for their belongings in the debris.

The Saturday after the Advance training ended, the entire Company was given twenty-four hour passes.

Carl, looking for a break from army life, decided he would take a campus tour of the University of Kansas, over at Lawrence. He was beginning to miss the tranquil hours spent studying, and the relaxed-pace of the university life.

In Junction City, he was walking to the Greyhound Bus station in the business section of town, when he saw Lasslett stepping out the door of a pawnshop. He wore civilian clothes.

"Hey," Carl shouted, "what you doing in a pawn shop?"

"Ah-h," Lasslett said when he recognized Carl. "I needed some cash," he said, walking up to Carl in his khaki uniform. "So I pawned our silverware -- a wedding gift from her mother and father."

Carl nodded.

"I bought a gun," Lasslett said quietly, near whispering.

"How come?" Carl said.

"Jackie says she heard someone around the trailer -- trying the back door," Lasslett said. "During the day. Now she's afraid -- for the baby."

"Maybe it was the gas-man," Carl said. "Somebody like that."

"No," Lasslett said. "She says she heard it yesterday again -- and with her step-mother gone home now -- she's really scared when I ain't around."

"Did you look around the park?" Carl said. "Maybe you can spot whoever --?"

"Whoever it is," Lasslett said, "knows I'm on duty at camp during the day -- that's for sure."

Lasslett shifted his weight from one leg to another.

"What kind of gun you get?" Carl said to break his nervousness.

"A little twenty-two," Lasslett said reaching into the pocket of his loose light-blue slacks.

He held out the tiny automatic in the palm of his hand showing it.

"How many shots?" Carl asked, smiling at the small size.

"Four bullets in the clip. And you can keep one more in the chamber if you want," Lasslett said, sliding the pistol back into his pocket. "But the pawn shop guy only had four twenty-twos left in the box of shells he had -- so that's all I got."

"That's the kind of gun," Carl said, "Jackie can slide under a pillow."

"Yeah," Lasslett said looking away, up the street. "Where you going?"

"I'm going to get a bus ticket -- go over to Lawrence," Carl said, looking in the direction of the Greyhound station. "I want to get away from the army -- for a while," he said, straightening his khaki tie -- "walk around the campus."

Lasslett grinned, and turned his head.

"Wish I had your problems," he said.

Carl nodded.

"You want to have a beer?" Lasslett asked.

"No, I want to get going."

"Well," Lasslett said, putting his hands in his pockets, "I got enough money left to buy a pint of gin -- I need some rest-and-relaxation too. Think I'll get some squirt for a mix -- make some Salty Dogs."

"Okay," Carl said stepping away. "See you around --"

"Oh," Lasslett said, "I forgot -- I'm being transferred back to Fox Company this week sometime."

"Yeah," Carl said, "I forgot too -- they want me to help put out the regimental newspaper, maybe. The Lieutenant in charge up there saw I studied journalism in college on my service records -- it's being hashed over -- I <u>might</u> be transferring to Regimental Headquarters Company.

"If I'm picked -- they could send me to a training school in New York -- for six weeks. New Rochelle, New York -- wherever the hell that is."

"No kidding," Lasslett said. "You wouldn't be in a shit-eating Line Company -- anymore."

"Ah," Carl said grinning, "there's nothing for sure. The Lieutenant just mentioned it to me when he was inspecting that bulletin board in the Mess Hall -- the one with all the stuff about Germany -- and where we're going -- and all that."

"You college guys," Lasslett said putting his hands in his pockets, "get all the breaks."

"There isn't nothing definite --" Carl said. "He might have forgot about the whole thing, that Lieutenant. Besides, the Company is under-strength -- guys are going to schools all over the place; tank mechanic school and stuff like that.

"The Company Commander will do everything to keep his people in the Company."

"Yeah," Lasslett said, "but <u>Orders From Headquarters</u>, buster, the Company Commander has to comply with."

"The whole thing is up in the air," Carl said. "It sounds too good to be true. I forgot the whole thing."

"You never know," Lasslett said, "what the Army is going to do." He took a step, then turned, "Hey, later maybe you want to stop by the trailer -- we're in twenty-seven."

"Twenty-seven," Carl said, "and Salty-dogs."

He watched Lasslett walking away quickly.

*   *   *   *   *

Stepping off the bus in Lawrence, Carl got no lift looking at the gray-stone buildings of the University of Kansas. It only raised his nostalgia level for the Detroit campus back home.

It was the same letdown he felt when he took the walk on Fort Riley, to see the "Geographical Center of the United States." The marker with a brass plaque was just a pile of rocks to him. But he thought he must see it.

The same thing happened in Florida, on the trip to Key West. There was a giant cement cone with the words: SOUTHERNMOST POINT OF THE UNITED STATES.

"I should have know," he said sitting down on a park bench in Lawrence, "this kind of stuff is for tourists -- not for guys in the army."

"Tourists are looking for something to do -- kill time. But guys in the Army don't live with time of their own -- the army takes most of it."

Getting up quickly off the bench, he started to the bus station for a ticket back to Junction City. He hoped Lasslett had not drunk all that quart of gin.

"Twenty-seven," he said going through the door of the station, "trailer twenty-seven."

It was just getting dark, when Lasslett opened the door of the trailer, wearing a sweatshirt with WISCONSIN in red letters on the front.

"Ah-ha, Carl," he said in a too loud voice, as if deliberately showing he was drunk. "Come in -- come in."

"Any gin left?" Carl said, "or am I too late?"

"Nah," he said backing up, "I just put a dent in it -- there's better than half left."

Then turning his head to the back of the narrow living room, he shouted in an overly loud voice, "Jackie -- we got company. Come see."

Carl suddenly felt he made a mistake coming here, as he climbed the wooden steps.

When Jackie came into the living room wiping her face with her hand, Carl knew he was intruding on something personal. She had been crying, but said, "Hello."

Carl could not stop looking at her shape. She wore shorts and a baggy pink shirt. He could not help seeing how her bare breasts sloped down to points under the shirt.

"Plunk it here --" Lasslett said waiving an open hand at the couch.

Carl sat down on the end of the couch that ran the length of the wall of the narrow room. He sat down, suddenly thinking he needed an excuse to leave, and said, "I was just going to the -- Cottontail Club Bar. I thought you might want to -- come along - for a while."

"Yeah," Jackie said sitting down on the opposite end of the couch from Carl, "take him for a walk -- cool him off."

"There's no hurry," Lasslett shouted, stepping behind the counter at the end of the room that formed the kitchen section of the trailer.

When Lasslett poured gin from the quart bottle, Carl saw it was near empty, as he filled two glasses.

To try and change the dark mood in the room, Carl said, "Hey, where'd you get that college sweatshirt?"

"It's mine," Jackie said. "I went to college in Madison for a year, but I didn't go back -- after my dad had a heart attack. I stayed home to help my stepmother manage the dairy -- until dad recovered."

"What were you studying?" Carl asked.

"Theater Arts," she said quietly. "I wanted to act."

When Lasslett handed him a drink and sat down between them on the couch, Carl said, "Sorry to show up -- unexpected -- but there wasn't much to see on campus -- over in Lawrence."

He said it to both of them.

"Madison is beautiful in the fall," Jackie said.

"I should have went to college," Lasslett said, "but I don't think I'd fit in. I've seen too much."

"Lawrence is one shade of gray," Carl said, sipping the drink, finding it mostly gin.

"I'll let you two talk," Jackie said. "It's near feeding time for the baby -- I have to go to the bedroom," she said getting up from the couch.

She seemed to be in a somber mood, Carl thought, not bouncy like she was in the PX cafeteria.

He watched her shorts and round rump go into the hallway.

"What you mean 'gray?'" Lasslett said and took a drink. "You said Lawrence campus was 'gray.'"

"Maybe it's just me," Carl said slowly, looking at his glass of gin, "but <u>everything</u> seemed gray -- the buildings -- the walls -- the streets."

Lasslett stood up and went to the back counter, and pouring more gin into his glass, said, grinning, "You been in the Army too long; you need a change."

He did not offer more gin to Carl.

"<u>Any time</u> in the army," Carl said, "is <u>too long</u>."

They both laughed.

Lasslett came back and dropped into the plastic lounge chair near the door, across from where Carl was sitting.

"Jackie's father and stepmother," he said slowly, a little slurred, "don't want her going to Germany with the baby."

Carl nodded, thinking that must be what they were squabbling about; he suddenly felt the guilt of intruding.

Looking for an excuse to break the mood, he said, "I have to tap a kidney." He did not want to hear marital problems.

Lasslett pointed to the hallway, "Right back to the end door -- is the bippy."

Carl finished his gin, and setting the empty glass on the kitchen counter as he walked, said, "Back in a flash."

When Carl stepped out of the bathroom, he saw Lasslett standing in the bedroom doorway, talking to his wife sitting on the bed.

"We're just going to the Cottontail Club," he said, Carl heard, "and shoot some pool -- for a while."

"Not too long," she said, Carl heard. "I'm afraid when it's dark."

"No more than an hour," he said in a voice that Carl noticed. He had trouble forming the words. "I promise, babe."

He backed out of the bedroom, and closing the door, whispered to Carl, "She only had a dollar and seventy-nine cents in change. You got any dough?"

"About seven bucks," Carl said in a low voice.

"That's enough," Lasslett said. "We're just going to the Cottontail Club -- four blocks over."

Carl nodded, smiling.

Going out the trailer door into the night air, Carl felt sure he smelled marijuana smoke in the bathroom.

Walking on the sidewalk in town under the streetlights, Carl was pulling his uniform tie up, listening to Lasslett's story about last week on the rifle range.

"The sun was blistering hot," Lasslett said, "and these two guys in the company, pulling and marking targets downrange, took off their fatigue shirts, then their t-shirts.

"And they got sunburned -- real bad -- red as lobsters."

Lasslett shifted the quart of gin in the paper bag from his left hand to his right, bunching up the WISONCSIN lettering on his sweatshirt.

The bar owner refused Lasslett drinking in the bar for being drunk already, but sold him the quart of gin to take home.

"And now," Lasslett said as they stopped walking at the curb of a narrow side street, "the Army wants to Court Martial them," he said waiving his free arm.

"Right," Carl said smiling, "because they were unfit for duty -- with hurting from the sunburn."

"Yep," Lasslett shouted. "Unfit for duty -- through negligence."

They both laughed, and stepping off the curb, Lasslett fell to his knees.

Carl was pulling him up by his free arm, when Lasslett said, "You know what Jackie said?"

He was back to talking about his argument with her, the reason he was drinking so much, and Carl made a sour face -- not wanting to hear what he would say next.

"She said, 'That's all I get? Two days in a motel -- I thought I'd get a honeymoon -- in Honolulu.'"

Carl turned his face away in an attempt not to hear more; then he saw the police car driving slowly up the curb behind them.

"Watch it," Carl said, "a cop car is behind us -- coming up."

"Ah, screw the cops," Lasslett said sliding the gin bottle bag under his baggy sweatshirt.

When the policeman stepped out of the car, Carl saw the Sergeant strips on his arm.

"Have you been drinking?" he asked Lasslett. "I saw you stumble -- off the curb."

"We had a few drinks at the trailer," Carl said quietly. "We just went to the store."

"Screw you," Lasslett shouted. "Can't a guy have a drink in his own damn house?"

"Come with me -- you're under arrest for Public Drunkenness," the Sergeant said taking hold of Lasslett's arm.

When the policeman pulled open the back door of the car to put Lasslett in the back seat, he pulled away.

"Carl," he shouted, "here -- take the bottle."

"No you don't," the Sergeant said, and pushed Lasslett hard, so his neck was caught between the door and the top of the car.

Lasslett choking, tried to get his arms up, and the bottle of gin slipped down from under the sweatshirt, hitting the pavement in a dull <u>wump</u> sound.

"Shit," Lasslett shouted, his face going red in the struggle.

"Get into that back seat -- now," the Sergeant shouted, pushing down on Lasslett.

Slowly, he dropped onto the back seat, lying on his side.

Carl stood watching them drive away, wondering why he was not arrested too.

"Maybe it's the uniform," he said.

For a moment, he stood looking at the wet spot where the bottle in the bag broke on the pavement.

"Poor bastard," he said, shaking his head. "I should go tell his wife -- so she can go bail him out."

Then he thought of the gun Lasslett bought for her.

"She might get scared," he said out loud, "if I show up at the door of the trailer. She might even shoot me -- to protect the baby."

He turned slowly, walking up the block to the bus stop for a ride back to camp.

"He'll call her from jail," he said, walking. "I don't want to see any more trouble tonight."

CHAPTER 5

GERMANY

Carl and Private Flannery were walking in the snow toward the PX. It was two days after New Years; the Regiment had been in Bamberg since the week before Thanksgiving, crossing the Atlantic on a troop ship, landing at Bremerhaven.

"So the major comes out of the Colonel's office," Flannery said grinning wide, "and he stands there at the closed door, wiping his eyes with a handkerchief; he had just been chewed out bad."

"He's pretty old," Carl said, "to be a major -- I mean he's got some white hair."

They were walking on the cobblestone road that circled the Regimental Headquarter parade grounds, in front of the building, with what looked like a giant onion on top the cupola, above the third floor.

Bamberg was thirty-nine kilometers west of the Czechoslovakian border.

"He's been passed over for promotion so many times," Flannery said flapping his arms against the cold, "that it isn't even funny."

They were dressed in their Class-A wool uniforms, with the short Eisenhower jacket, but did not have on overcoats.

"Anyhow," Flannery said, talking from the side of his mouth in his usual manner, "I'm reading Playboy -- out flat in my desk drawer in front of me -- that I can close on the double if any officers come by my desk --"

"Ah-h," Carl said, "the major is good at planning stuff they do at G-3."

"Okay," Flannery says while pushing his army steel eyeglasses up on his nose, "so the major says, 'I know I'm not as smart as some people -- but I try hard.'"

"He really said that?" Carl asked smiling.

"I tried to keep from busting out laughing," Flannery said. "I wanted to crawl in my desk drawer before I exploded. But I kept my head down, and bit my lip, until I got over wanting to laugh."

"You got to feel for the old major," Carl said. "Why they didn't leave him back at Ft. Riley -- I can't figure."

"The army has to use what it's got," Flannery said as they turned past the piles of snow outside the PX doorway.

Carl and Flannery could both type, and were sent from Fox Company to help at Regimental Headquarters with all the paperwork that had to be typewritten.

When they heard the Colonel would be out of his office for the rest of the day, they would sneak away from their desks.

Carl, following Flannery, stepped into the cafeteria line at the PX, picking up a plastic tray.

"Rumor has it," Flannery said speaking out the side of his mouth as he usually did, "the Colonel is going to close the cafeteria at noon."

"How come?" Carl asked, sliding his tray on the rails along the food counter.

He was watching the trim woman director of the cafeteria section walk out of her office, behind the food counter. She wore a long white lab coat, and looked more like a doctor than a food service employee. She was a German, clearly over-educated for the job she held, Carl thought.

Flannery was at the coffee urn, holding a cup under the spigot, watching the glow to turn the spigot closed.

"Seems everybody is boycotting the food in the Mess Hall at noon," he said. "The cooks are complaining -- so the Colonel might make the cafeteria -- on duty days -- at noon -- off limits."

"Yeah," Carl said, filling his coffee cup, "for a quarter -- you can get a hamburger here -- and that beats that Mess Hall stuff, any day."

"How are you today?" a voice asked from behind Carl.

When he turned around, Carl faced Father Bennett, the Catholic Regimental Chaplain.

"We're doing -- pretty good, Father," Carl said, feeling uneasy about how to talk to a priest, socially. "I mean -- we're as good as can be expected --"

"Morning Father," Flannery blurted over Carl's shoulder. "Join us at a table?"

"Certainly," the Priest said, stopping as Carl reached at the last moment to take a twisted doughnut with cinnamon.

Already at the table, next to the large window overlooking the snowy Parade Ground outside, where the same people who usually sat together were, was the soldier Nathanson. He claimed to be a Harvard grad, and was talking to a guy who said he was a lawyer from Massachusetts, who Carl knew only by his last name that rhymed with Mazola Oil.

Carl, sitting down at the table, heard Private Nathanson saying to the lawyer, "In Paris, the French have adopted our 'La Hot Dog' but they abhor the hamburger."

Carl, listening for more, sliding his doughnut and coffee off the tray, silently, heard Nathanson say, "The French think grinding up beef -- is barbaric. The hamburger will never catch on in Paris."

Putting his empty tray on a chair, Carl saw a soldier talking to the Priest at the end of the cafeteria line, and they were deeply engrossed in conversation.

Flannery, sitting across the table from Carl, holding his coffee cup in both hands, said, "I went to Frankfort last weekend -- and I found out Elvis drinks at the Fisherstube. The German girls -- and some American over here with their Army families -- all line up for a block from the bar -- just to get a look at him."

Carl, nodding, said to Flannery, "I want to do some traveling too -- I even bought that mimeograph pamphlet from the PX bookrack, <u>A GI's Guide to Europe,</u> that gives the cheap places to sleep and eat."

Over Flannery's shoulder, Carl could see another soldier standing with the priest now, waiting to talk with him when the first soldier was done.

"Did you hear what happened in Darmstadt on the Armed Forces Network radio program?" Flannery asked, setting down his cup.

When Carl shook his head, Flannery said, "Some guys from an Engineer Unit called in on the request hour to Munich -- during the 'Luncheon in Munchin Hour' -- and asked for the record 'You Ain't Nothing' But a Hound Dog,' dedicated to their Company Commander."

"No kidding?" Carl said, grinning, taking a bite of his twisted doughnut.

"Yeah," Flannery said, hunching forward over the table, "so the Company Commander calls the radio station and says -- the whole company is restricted to barracks until further notice."

"That's crazy," Carl said before taking another bite of his doughnut, smiling, shaking his head.

"I heard someplace, Rosemary Clooney's brother is the announcer for the radio station -- there in Munich," Carl added.

Nodding, Flannery said, "I can top that. Bing Crosby's twin sons are Mail Clerks at Division Headquarters in Wurzburg -- Phillip and Dennis, I think, is their names."

"They should call it -- 'Wurzburg Celebrity Mail'" -- the lawyer said, and Carl and Flannery looked at one another, stunned; he had been listening to what they were saying.

The priest came over, carrying his cup of coffee on a saucer, "Mind if I join the merriment here?" he said sitting down.

Behind him came Private Lonsdale -- the projectionist for the base movie theatre. Carl knew him from his day work, cranking the mimeograph machine -- printing duplicates of orders -- in the basement of Regimental Headquarters. Carl would take the typed stencils down to Lonsdale to be printed.

"What's the movie tonight?" Flannery asked Lonsdale.

"Picnic" Lonsdale said, stirring his hot chocolate in a tall paper cup, "with Kim Novak, and -- a --"

"William Holded," the lawyer said.

"I haven't seen you boys in chapel," the priest said quietly to Flannery and Carl.

"We've been working Sundays -- sometimes," Flannery said. "But we'll try to be at chapel this Sunday."

"We have to get back to the office, Father," Carl said, "G-3 is a busy place. The phones are always ringing."

When he stood up, Carl saw a balding spot at the top of the priest's black hair.

"Bye, Father," Flannery said getting up from the table. "We'll be seeing you."

"Soon, I hope," the priest said, looking at his coffee that had cooled.

Outside, walking in the snow, Carl said, "I'm really tempted to type an overnight pass -- and put it in front of the Lieutenant -- he signs everything I set in front of him. He don't even read it."

"What if he catches you?" Flannery said, shaking himself to get warm.

"He'd probably laugh."

"Yeah, he's like that," Flannery said, folding his arms across his chest. "I hear he's supposed to be promoted to Captain -- real soon."

"He was in the fighting in Korea," Carl said. "I've heard him talking to other officers -- on nights when I'm on CQ. They ask him about the war."

When they started up the steps of the headquarters building, Carl added, "I've heard him talk about 'cleaning out a bunker' full of Chinese and North Koreans."

A Corporal that Carl knew from Fox Company was coming out the headquarters door.

"Breckles," the Corporal said, "the First Sergeant sent me to find you -- nobody knows where you are, since they transferred you up here to G-3."

"I bunk here at the Regimental Headquarters Company," Carl said, defensively. "What does the First Sergeant want?"

Flannery hit Carl's arm, saying, "I'm going up to the office."

"Lasslett asked the First Sergeant to send for you," the Corporal said, "so I hear Lasslett wants to talk to you."

"Why don't Lasslett come himself?"

"He's in detention."

Carl watched the door behind the Corporal close slowly, after Flannery went inside.

"Detention for what?" Carl asked folding his arms.

"A Court Martial." Carl was looking at the nametag on the Corporal's chest: BOIKE. "They're holding him in a room in the barracks -- they use for storage. They put him in there after the fight -- some windows were broke, chairs smashed up."

"What are they charging him with?"

"I don't know for sure," Boike said. "The Sergeant just said Lasslett wants to talk to you about the trail."

"Okay, I'll come over -- when I get off duty."

"Right," Boike said, turning away, going down the steps.

*　　*　　*　　*　　*

It was snowing hard when Carl came out of the Mess Hall, and it was growing dark.

Walking down the steps, he overheard two soldiers behind him talking, "I can feel that stew for dinner -- burning in my gut already."

"Wait to later," a second soldier said. "It gets worse."

Carl grinned at the wisecrack, knowing it to probably be true, hunched his shoulders against the cold, while walking down the row of two-story barracks buildings; he had been putting off going to consult with Lasslett long enough.

Someone said the German troops from these same <u>Warner Cascerne</u> barracks were the ones who marched into Czechoslovakia in 1939.

Carl could see the rings still on the walls that faced the roadway, where the military horses were tethered in the old days; it was history he thought, but it was not a good history.

Inside the barracks, the Charge-of-Quarters came out of the first floor office; it was Corporal Boike again.

"Lasslett is down the hall -- at the end," Boike said leading the way for Carl, who was brushing the wet snow off his shoulder. "I got to unlock the door."

When the door swung open, Carl saw Lasslett sitting on a bunk bed at the end of the room, a single light hanging overhead.

"I was wondering if you'd come," Lasslett said, not getting up from the unmade bunk, but leaning forward, his elbows on his knees.

"Knock when you want out," Boike said, swinging the door closed, locking it from the outside.

Carl looked at the stack of mattresses, rolled and tied with rope, against the right wall, a desk with all the drawers missing, and a cabinet with the door hanging loose, and said, "How did you manage to get here? I mean, what are you in detention for?"

Carl sat down on the desk without drawers, and sliding back, dangled his legs.

Before Lasslett could speak, Carl said, "You seem to spend a lot of time in jails -- detention."

"I was lucky in Junction City," Lasslett said sitting up straight, "the judge let me out -- two days before the troop train left Fort Riley for New York.

"You bring anything to drink?" he said, tipping up his hand like he was drinking a beer.

"Not this time," Carl said, wiping the wet from the snow off his face. "Next time. Now tell me what they got you here for."

"My wife flew Lufthansa to Frankfort, and took a train here to Bamberg -- three days ago," Lasslett said leaning on his elbows again. "I went to help her settle in at the apartment I found in town -- I spent that day with her -- and I stayed all night.

"I missed Company Roll Call the next morning -- so they got me for AWOL."

"That don't sound too bad," Carl said, noticing now in the dull light, Lasslett had not been shaving. He had a stubble on his face, and the shirt he wore had stains down the front.

Lasslett took out a cigarette from his shirt pocket, and lighting it, said, "The Company Commander says I knew all about how the army is discouraging enlisted men from bringing their wives over here to Germany." Blowing out smoke he added, "Cause we're going to be in the field -- camping out -- eight or nine months out of the year -- on the field training exercises."

"So why do they have you in this store room?" Carl asked, then noticed the broken window behind Lasslett that was hidden before, the outside shutter closed, making the window dark. "You do that?" Carl asked pointing.

"Yeah," Lasslett said, nodding. "They said I was confined to quarters until the trail -- and I wanted to go to town -- we had a fight."

"Okay," Carl said, "I heard there was a fight before I got here -- but, why you telling me all this? I mean, what can I do about this?"

Lasslett, looking at the cigarette in his hand, said, "I want you to talk for me -- at the Court Martial -- represent me. You've been to college, Carl. You're smarter than me," Lasslett said, dropping his cigarette on the floor, where there were a dozen crushed butts already, and stepped on it.

"No," Carl said, leaning back to straighten upright on the desk, "I can't do that. What if you end up at the Big Eight prison in Mannheim? It would be all my fault."

"What's the difference?" Lasslett said leaning forward, elbows on his knees again. "That's where I'm going to end up anyway -- Mannheim Army Prison."

"All right," Carl said. "All right, I get the message." Leaning forward, he said, "Let me think about it -- but I'm not going to make any promises right now."

"Okay," Lasslett said looking straight at Carl, "that's why I asked them to bring you here."

"You've really put a load on me," Carl said sliding off the desktop.

Lasslett smiled; he knew Carl would not refuse.

Walking over to the door, knocking, Carl said back to Lasslett, "Clean this place up, and shave. Quit acting like a maniac -- you're acting like they want you to act --"

"Right," Lasslett said standing up, "I see what you mean."

* * * * *

At the coffee table in the PX cafeteria the next morning, Carl sat down in the chair next to the lawyer.

Private Nathanson, sitting on the other side of the lawyer, said, "Ah, if it isn't the regimental dissipating romantic," as he leaned forward to talk to Carl, around the lawyer.

"Yes," Carl said. "And I owe it all to a fondness for cognac."

"You're becoming a drinking legend in Bamberg," Nathanson quipped.

"Too bad I didn't attend Harvard," Carl said. "Now let me talk to my lawyer, legends are not without problems."

"I can well imagine, Breckles," Nathanson said quietly, but leaned back, not saying any more.

"Maybe you can help me with a legal problem," Carl said to the lawyer, who had been listening while pouring cream into his coffee.

"I'll help -- if I can," the lawyer said, looking around the table at the others talking. "It all depends on what the legal problem is."

"I've got a friend in Fox Company, who the Army is Court Martialling for AWOL," Carl said, looking around the table; the priest was not here today.

The lawyer nodded, listening closely to Carl, and when Carl hesitated, took a drink of coffee.

"Well," Carl said, resting his elbows on the table, and crossing his hands in front of his face, "My friend's wife flew over from the States a few days ago -- he went in to Bamberg when she got here by train -- to help her settle in the apartment he had rented. She has a baby with her.

"And to make a long story short, my friend, Michael Lasslett, stayed the night -- and in the morning, missed Roll Call at Fox Company."

Carl watched the lawyer set his coffee cup slowly down on the saucer.

"Is Absent Without Leave the only thing he is charged with?" the lawyer asked.

"As far as I know, yes," Carl said slowly, thinking. "I need some way to beat this AWOL thing," he added. He wants me to -- act as his -- lawyer. Speak for him. I don't know where to begin."

The lawyer was scratching his forehead, absent-minded, just above his right eyebrow.

"Maybe," Carl said rotating his empty cup on the saucer, "you might -- talk to him -- maybe represent him at the Court Martial."

The lawyer was silent, then leaning back in his chair, said, "What's your friend's name again -- over there in Fox Company?"

"Just ask for Lasslett," Carl said. "They guy in detention."

*   *   *   *   *

After Lasslett was found not guilty at the Court Martial, Carl heard the guys from Fox Company saying they were going to find a lawyer -- if they were ever hauled in before one. Some, who were facing Court Martials, were out looking for people in camp with legal training.

Then the Company Commander had a notice put on the Company bulletin board, that the Colonel had written a directive saying that no lawyers would be permitted in the future to speak for soldiers appearing before Court Martial hearings.

Carl, fearing he would be connected with Lasslett getting off, stayed away from Fox Company. He stayed away from the PX also.

He was not feeling too well and began sleeping much more; laying out on his made-up bed in the Headquarters barracks, in full uniform, afternoons, to take a nap.

He felt tired all the time, and thought he needed more rest.

After a week, he learned about the trail that the lawyer questioned the First Sergeant closely -- if he had actually walked to the place where Private Lasslett was assigned to stand in the ranks.

It is dark in the morning when the Company falls-out for Roll Call, and the First Sergeant answered "No," that he had just heard Lasslett was missing, and reported it.

The officers hearing the testimony then dismissed the case.

Carl waited two weeks before going back to the PX, and on the afternoon he walked in for coffee, spotted the lawyer sitting at the table.

Sitting down across the table, Carl asked quietly, "Can we pay you something -- for legal fees?"

"No," the lawyer said, shaking his head, looking at the others around the table, to see if they were listening, "it was something I did to help out Lasslett and his wife."

Carl sipped coffee, and then setting the cup down, said, "You won't have any trouble -- in civilian life -- making a living as an attorney."

He meant it as a compliment; that people would talk about a -- sympathetic -- lawyer for their problems, and go to him for help.

"I want to be a judge," the lawyer said smiling, showing a gap between his two front teeth, "and someday -- run for Congress."

"You sure got things mapped out," Carl said lifting his cup. "I wish I was like that."

"Why does Nathanson call you a 'dissipate?'" the lawyer asked, showing the tooth-gap again.

"He saw me dancing with two girls at the Golden Lion one night. They were German girls, who had been riding on a motor scooter and were hit by a truck -- out in the farm country.

"One lost a foot, and she was on crutches, the other one had her leg in a cast."

"How could they dance?"

"Slowly," Carl said, leaning back in his chair, "and we had finished two bottles of cognac.

"The best part came later," Carl said grinning. "They have a loft -- they design clothes -- and want to go to Paris. They're wild -- when it comes to sex; everybody in the bar knows them."

The lawyer nodded, looking away -- out the wide window overlooking the snow-covered Parade Ground outside, smiling.

*   *   *   *   *

Three months later, springtime, the Directive the Colonel made about soldiers facing Court Martial proceedings, not permitting lawyers, was swept away.

Five black soldiers on the Regimental Boxing Team were arrested and charged with raping a German girl.

The camp grapevine story was the boxers were training, running on the paths in the woods near Bamberg, when they came across the German girl and her boyfriend -- making love.

Some of the boxers, advancing on her asked to make love, and they said she consented, so the grapevine story went. But after, she demanded money for her services.

They were wearing sweatpants, so they had no wallets. When she got no money -- she yelled rape.

Civil Rights leaders began showing up in Bamberg for the Court Martial; the Army penalty for rape is death by hanging.

When Adam Clayton Powell, the Congressman from Harlem showed up in Frankfort, it made international news, that he had come to hear the trail.

No one was hanged, but after the Court Martial, some of the five boxers went to jail.

A movie was made, with a different scenario than what actually happened in Bamberg, and a popular song was written. Both had the title, "A Town Without Pity," but this all came two years later.

CHAPTER 6

When Sergeant Bowman walked into the G-3 office in Regimental Headquarters, Carl looked across to Flannery at his desk and shrugged.

The Sergeant First Class was the manager of the Enlisted Men's Club in the three-story building next to the Warner Caserne camp entrance gate.

The Club occupied the entire ground floor of the building; there was a central bar that served the tables where the hostess German girls carried drinks to the men.

Across the wide aisle way from the table was a dance floor with a bandstand. Up at the front of the club that faced the street outside was a lounge with rugs, sofas, overstuffed chairs, and a jukebox.

The Club was a place where off-duty soldiers could relax after the flag was taken down in the evening.

"How you doing, there?" the Sergeant said to Carl with a wide smile.

Carl grinned back, looking at his chubby face, and stomach that protruded, pushing out his short Eisenhower jacket in front. Carl looked at Flannery, as if to ask what he did last night to cause the jovial mood the Sergeant was in. Flannery shrugged.

"I'm a little hung over," Carl said, "but -- I'll live."

Sergeant Bowman walked over to the desk where Carl sat at a typewriter.

"Boy, you sure were funny last night, kid. You had everybody in stitches with your joking -- the whole table was laughing themselves silly."

Carl leaned back in his chair for relief, listening.

"That joke about the spastic kid," Sergeant said, hands on his hips, "and how he hit his forehead with the ice-cream cone -- his tongue out -- like this --"

Carl watched as the Sergeant stuck out his tongue, and moved his hand like he was trying to put the cone in his mouth, but like the spastic kid, missed the mouth, and splashed the ice cream cone on his forehead.

The Sergeant was laughing, Carl smiling, when suddenly the Major came out of the Colonel's office. He was carrying a folder, open, reading the papers inside, and slowly walked to his office, without looking up.

"Okay," Carl said to the Sergeant, "We got a backlog of work here today -- there's a pile of typing to do -- and"

"Yeah, and I've got to get to work too over in the club," Sergeant Bowman said turning sideways. "I came here to ask you to come by tonight -- join us at the big table -- tell some more jokes for the people. It's good for business, and that's <u>my</u> job.

"And your drinks are on the club."

Carl looked across to Flannery at his desk and saw an exaggerated long face.

"Okay," Carl said looking up at the Sergeant, speaking quietly, "I'll stop by later -- and bum a few drinks."

When the Sergeant went out the door, Carl said over to Flannery, "What you think of that offer? Free drinks, wow."

Flannery tilted his head, and looking out the office window, said, "I don't know -- I don't know --" and Carl sensed he did not want to answer.

"Yeah," Carl said, "that's what I'm thinking too. It sounds -- fishy -- or something. Free drinks -- of all things, that's hard to pass up, I mean -- I hate to say no."

Flannery waived his arms apart, "Try it out. Then you'll know for sure what it's all about."

"Yeah," Carl said. "That's what I can do."

Later, when they were both coming out of the Fox Company Mess Hall, Master Sergeant Brenner was coming up the walkway. His arms were near covered with chevrons and service stripes; he ran the company's day-to-day business and looked it.

"I was just coming up to headquarters to talk to you two," he said, watching Flannery pulling down on his uniform jacket to straighten it. "You're both transferred to Headquarter Company to work as clerks. Permanently.

"Your orders are being cut at the Company, and you will both get copies."

"Should we move our equipment over?" Carl asked.

"No," the Sergeant said, as another soldier passed them on the walkway, the Sergeant waiting until he was out of earshot, "they don't have room at Headquarters Company barracks. We found you billeting at the Troop Education and Information Section -- in the building next door.

"Report to a Sergeant Sikorsky for your bed assignments."

Carl and Flannery both nodded without looking at one another.

"Turn in your field equipment to the Fox Company Supply Sergeant, and draw new stuff at Headquarters Company," Brenner said before walking off down the sidewalk.

Watching him go, Carl, smiling, raising his eyebrows, said, "How's that for a stroke of luck?"

Flannery, grinning back, said, "I wonder if they have a barracks bed-check?"

"Who cares," Carl said, punching him on the shoulder. We'll practically be on our own -- from now on."

The Troop Education Section held classes for soldiers who wanted to get a GED diploma, a high school equivalent, or even take nightly classes from the University of Maryland extension service, that were taught here.

The soldiers who taught the classes were all high school certified teachers. Their barracks was located upstairs on the floor above the classrooms and offices.

*   *   *   *   *

"<u>Fasching</u>?" Carl asked, looking around the table at the enlisted Men's Club, where the same groups of people had been gathering to drink for over two weeks. Some were Germans.

Carl had just arrived at the club and took a chair next to Margerite, looking at the people wearing party hats, some dressed in costumes.

"It is like the Mardi Gras," Margerite said in her clipped English, straightening her pointed paper hat. "The German festival -- before Lent begins.

"People do a lot of drinking -- dress in silly costumes. They will not celebrate again -- until Lent ends."

Margerite was a thin German woman, who sold jewelry, some of it made of sea-shells, from a display table back near the opening in the wall to the kitchen. Soldiers could buy hamburgers and french-fries from the kitchen that was in the rear of the Club.

Carl saw that the Fasching party was ending -- the dance floor empty. The few soldiers who had been drinking beer did not seem interested in Fasching; it was a German holiday, but they had sat watching the celebrating.

The women waitresses, cleaning up the tables and floor, still wore their party hats, as they worked closing down the Club for the night.

Twenty minutes ago, before Carl arrived, Sergeant Bowman, dressed in a double-breasted grey suit, a paper hat in the shape of a derby on his head, had his picture taken with the entire Club staff, all in party costumes, the band included.

Rudi, the German drummer with the band, sat opposite Carl at the table. He was "tipsy" -- the polite German word for drunk -- and he had the letters RA painted on his forehead with lipstick.

Rudi, Carl noticed, always drank cheap German cognac when he joined the table after hours.

"You were Regular Army?" Carl asked Rudi, grinning, pointing at the letters on his forehead, then sipping from the half-full glass of vodka he held.

"I love the army," he said, a smile on his wide face. "I was in the artillery -- in the war." He took a quick sip of cognac, and said, "I wanted to join the Waffen SS -- the -- elite. But I did not qualify," Rudi said shaking his head slow.

"Well," Carl said looking at his vodka glass, "at least you didn't have to shoot anybody -- face-to-face -- I mean."

"I had a chance," Rudi said, leaning clumsily forward against the table. "In Cologne -- two Amees -- GIs came in a Jeep near me in a bombed house. I could shoot them both -- but I put my rifle down. The war was finished."

He leaned back and slowly sipped cognac.

Sergeant Bowman passed behind Rudi on the way back from depositing the club bar money in the safe. He unbuttoned his suit coat, and sat down at the head of the table.

"Rudi," he said, "you telling war stories again? I heard what you were telling Carl."

He was smiling, but there was no humor in his remark.

"Nothing the police -- should know," Rudi said, quickly.

"I used to be in the Military Police -- Criminal Investigation Division," he said, and it stunned the people at the table. He was flaunting authority -- as if being the Club Manager was not enough.

Carl, wanting to make a joke, lighten the atmosphere, said, "The Military Police -- is a military occupation I thoroughly disapprove of --"

He said it to Margerite sitting next to him, but she did not react; she sat turning the tulip-shaped glass of cognac with two fingers.

"In the States," Sergeant Bowman said continuing, "I used to be a guard at Leavenworth -- the military prison in Kansas."

Everyone at the table looked at him, wondering what he would say next.

"That's a hard place," Carl said. "That sounds like a fun-filled assignment."

"I just got in the Army," Bowman said, as if he did not hear, "and when I was making the rounds one night, a prisoner said he was going to commit suicide -- and he wanted two aspirin, now, because he had a headache."

"Why bother with the aspirin?" Carl said.

"I know," Sergeant Bowman said grinning, "so I said I'll give you aspirin -- if you don't commit suicide while I'm on duty. I don't want to fill out all the paperwork. He says 'okay', so I give him aspirin."

"Did he do it?" Carl asked, finishing the vodka in his glass, watching as the people around the table were looking away, uncomfortable.

"Yeah," Bowman said, "and he waited until the morning shift came on duty. They found him hanging in his cell, I heard later."

One of the waitresses began snapping out the overhead lights, at the far end of the long clubroom, making it dark.

"I feel like a party tonight," Sergeant Bowman said, while getting up from the table, buttoning his suit coat. "Let's all go to town -- all of us."

"I can't go," Carl said getting up from the table. "Private Sikorsky don't like it -- when I show up down in the hallway -- and clap my hands -- and he has to come down and unlock the gate to let me upstairs.

"He's our boss up there in the Education Center -- my barracks -- and after nine o'clock, I'm supposed to be in bed."

"A Private?" Bowman asked.

"Yeah," Carl said smiling, "he's the head teacher -- and he runs the show -- he's a mathematician. He lock up everything over there."

Margerite stood up, and she pressed her left hand on top of Carl's; he was surprised, he figured she and the Sergeant were in some kind of relationship.

"Don't worry about Private Sikorsky," Sergeant Bowman said to Carl, "I'll have a talk with him tomorrow -- explain your situation."

"I got no pass for town," Carl said, watching Margerite putting on her hat, thinking the wide brim made her look like Greta Garbo when it dropped over her eyes, "and the MPs will grab me."

"I'll take care of the MPs," Bowman said, looking around the clubroom as the final lights overhead went out. "C'mon everybody."

In the dim light, Margerite lifted her fur coat off the back of the chair, and Carl helped her pull it on as they were walking to the door with the others.

Carl slid his hand on her breast; Margerite continued walking calmly. He wanted more of her; she knew it now.

"You don't have to worry about the gate guard," Sergeant Bowman said to Carl following him going down the steps. "I got my Chevy -- the guards salute when I drive out the gate.

"They never check the people inside the car."

Carl grinned at what Bowman said about the car going out the gate with a salute; he had similar windfall at the Education Center two days ago.

He was going to the barracks to nap in the afternoon, and on the steps he met Keller, one of the teachers, going up to the Center. Carl thought he had a key, and stopped behind him and waited.

The gate was locked.

"Don't tell anybody," Keller whispered. Then he put his fingers through the fencing of the gate, as if grasping a handful, and shook the gate portion. The wave action of the gate separated the bolt out of the lock hasp, and the gate swung open.

"We don't want Sikorsky to know about this," Keller said.

"Don't worry," Carl remembered saying, "he sure won't."

Carl, realizing he could come and go from the barracks at any time, decided he would not even tell Private Flannery.

There would be no more clapping your hands, and waiting for a grumbling Private Sikorsky in a t-shirt to come downstairs and unlock the wire-fence gate late in the evening.

Another trick for getting back into camp late at night, a soldier told Carl about at the PX.

The German guard at the far end of the camp, beyond the tank park, could not read English, the soldier said. You could show him anything with printing on it -- even a library card -- and he would let you in camp.

The only drawback was that it was a long hike through the tank park, to get to the barracks.

There was yet another way into camp, Carl heard about, that grew out of the Colonel posting Special Police at the gate. These were not Military Police, but men from the Companies on guard duty.

They knew men from their outfit, who would have the taxi stop thirty yards short of the gate, pay the driver quickly, and make a run for the camp wall -- that was about seven or eight feet high -- and jump up, and pull themselves over.

Word about it spread fast, and soon everyone did it.

Sergeant Bowman was right. The first night Carl and the crowd from the table after the Fasching party rode in the Chevy out the gate, the guard saluted.

A light rain was falling, and it was dark, and Carl, sitting in the back seat of the car next to Margerite, thought the weather might have made them lucky.

Sitting up front in the car, between Sergeant Bowman and Rudi, was a young waitress, Irmgard, who had long black hair. She always wore tight sweaters, and it caught the Sergeant's eye.

She laughed at the things he said, and when he met her at the club door, going out, he invited her along.

Carl sat riding in the car, looking out at the dark cobblestone streets, shiny in the drizzle. Only the beer stubs were lit. Carl saw the Fasching celebration was going on, people were dancing outside the bars, some holding beer bottles.

At the street corner, Carl saw a man sitting on the curb, wearing a skeleton suit, the bones glowing white, and a woman with a pointed hat, wearing a witch costume, bending to talk to him.

"Where are we going?" Carl asked Sergeant Bowman, who was driving slow while near the revelers.

They were passing the Gableman statue in the town square, which looked like Neptune with a trident. Someone told Carl, he remembered, Bamberg was under siege in medieval times, and a water spring appeared where the statue was now, the city was saved -- they had water to last out the war.

"We go to the Salamander," Rudi said in a loud party voice without turning around.

"My wife works there -- we can get extra drinks free -- and we don't tip," he said and laughed.

CHAPTER 7

Margerite moved, uncomfortable, and pulled her fur coat collar up against her face.

Carl moved his arm across the top of the car seat, around her shoulders, and he felt her hip against his.

"The Salamander will be too crowded," Margerite said, softly. "It is Fasching -- everyone is -- celebrating there."

"Yeah," Carl said, "maybe we shouldn't be out too late tonight."

He suddenly felt guilty for being in town, and along with it, he was feeling tired again. Lately, the tired feeling was coming more often during the duty hours, and he was forced to lie down and rest. His chest felt heavy, like he had a cold.

Driving past the open double-doors of the Salamander Bar, Carl saw the crowd had spilled out onto the sidewalk. Inside he could see people dancing to the loud music. Most wore costumes.

"Must we go there?" Margerite said to everybody in the car, in the tone of a mild protest.

"We can try the Wallenstein Keller," Rudi said turning to look back at her for a moment. "Who knows for sure -- we might meet some of the Bamberg Symphony.

"Maybe you want to drink with that sort?"

"I don't like tipsy people falling on my table," Margerite said slowly.

"Reminds you too much of the Enlisted Men's Club -- on payday," Sergeant Bowman said driving, not looking back, "hey Margie."

"We can go to a place," the waitress, Imgard said to Bowman, calmly, "I know it is never crowded. I worked there for a year -- I know for sure."

"Where is it, shatz?" Rudi asked her.

"In English, the Happy Shepard," she said, "up in the hills -- you can see the Altmann Schloss across the way."

"The Happy Shepard," Rudi said, "I know it -- it is a gasthaus -- it's for tourists."

"Yes," Irmgard said turning to Rudi, "it is not just for drinking -- you must eat something also."

"We should go there," Margerite said, in a relieved voice, "just for tonight, so we don't see all the drinking and craziness."

"Okay," Sergeant Bowman said, "we'll go there. What the hell. Show me the road."

"That road ahead," Rudi said pointing, "it goes to the left, and up in the hills."

Carl kissed the side of Margerite's face in the dark, and when she turned, kissed her lips, and was surprised at her eagerness.

It seemed unusual to Carl, a woman working in a Club, who was attractive, soldiers all around, starved for affection. It did not add up, Carl thought, she must get a hundred propositions a week.

And Sergeant Bowman, Carl figured he must have the inside track to her, but they did not act like they were interested in one another. He had been watching for signs.

When the steep road ended, and the car headlights fell on the gasthaus across the flat courtyard, the building was dark.

"Looks like everybody is sleeping," Bowman said, stopping.

"The owner," Irmgard said motioning for Rudi to open the car door, "Frau Runge, sleeps upstairs -- she is a widow.

"She will open for customers -- she does it often. But you must buy things to eat. She cooks for the patrons -- to make her money."

"I could use some ham and eggs," Bowman said walking up to the dark entrance door.

Irmgard knocked firmly on the door, and when a tall woman with white hair appeared under the overhead light, the two had a brief conversation in German, then the woman, pulling her green bathrobe closed further, swung the heavy door open.

"Workmen are painting the guest dining room," Irmgard said to everyone entering through the door. "Frau Runge says we are to use the large table in the kitchen -- this way," she said pointing past a stuffed bear standing upright.

"She will join us in the kitchen -- she is dressing."

"I need a drink real bad," Sergeant Bowman said following Irmgard who snapped on the lights in the kitchen.

She went out, pulling off her raincoat.

There was a giant bottle of cognac on a swivel in the center of the table, and glasses off to the side. Everyone was filling their glasses and taking seats in the heavy wood chairs.

"How old is Irmgard?" Rudi asked Bowman while tilting the bottle in its rack, holding the neck, to fill his glass.

"Seventeen," Bowman said quietly. "But the worst of it -- so I hear -- she's pregnant."

Carl, waiting to fill his glass, said "We better order another bottle of cognac -- if we want to drown our troubles."

"At home," Sergeant Bowman said to Rudi, "my wife is accusing me of flirting with the young maid we hired to do the housework. When I don't come home tonight -- I'm really going to be in the doghouse."

"Cognac won't help you much with troubles," Margerite said sitting down in a chair, slipping her coat off her shoulders.

Irmgard came back into the room, followed by Frau Runge.

"I ordered ham and eggs for us all," she said to Sergeant Bowman. "Does anyone want potatoes?"

"Yes," Rudi said, "something to absorb the cognac."

Frau Runge smiled pulling open the large refrigerator.

Carl, sipping cognac, suddenly felt nauseated; something was wrong. The cognac seemed to bite, harshly, there was no warm feeling from it.

He choked.

"What is the matter?" Margerite asked him. "You look pale, Carl -- are you sick?"

He was shaking his head, when his stomach rejected the alcohol, making him wretch.

Covering his mouth, he asked, "Where is the bathroom?"

Irmgard pointed, "At the end of the hall there."

"I'll come with you Carl," Margerite said getting up from her chair.

"No, no," Carl said putting his hand on her shoulder as he stood up. "I'll be all right in a minute. I just want to put cold water on my face."

"If you need -- help -- call me," Margerite said softly while sitting back down.

Carl stopped in the hall and lurched through a doorway. When he snapped on the light, he found it was not the bathroom, but a study. On the desk in front of him was the photograph of a young German soldier. It showed him from the waist up, the swastika and eagle badge of the Wehrmacht on his chest.

A long stem red rose lay at the bottom of the photograph frame.

"That picture could be anyone," Carl said. "He must be dead -- the flower."

"All armies are the same," he said, snapping off the light, stepping back into the hallway. "The families are the ones who pay the price."

In the bathroom, Carl splashed water on his face in the sink, and when he straightened up, the heaving stomach started again, at first dry, then a forceful wretch brought up what was in his stomach. There was not much fluid, but it was streaked with pink.

"Could be that Mess Hall chili at lunch," he said, wiping his mouth, rinsing out the washbasin.

Looking in the mirror, he saw his face pale, drawn.

"Maybe the bile is just cognac," he said to himself in the mirror. "My system -- is just rejecting the alcohol."

Back in the kitchen at the table, Carl sat down listening to Sergeant Bowman telling a story.

"And the Colonel and the major were inspecting the K-9 Guard Dogs in formation out front of Regimental Headquarters," Bowman said holding out one hand.

"Then, one of the dogs lunged as they walked past, and the Colonel grabbed the old major by the shoulders," Bowman said, using both hands like he was holding the major, "and he shoves the old major in front of the dog -- and skips away."

Bowman laughed and so did Rudi, who slapped the table.

"Carl," Margerite said quietly, "your face looks so white." She was leaning from her chair next to him. "Are you -- all right?"

"I'm okay, really. I'm just tired," he said, and to change the subject, asked, "what happened to Frau Runge's husband?" He looked over at her working at the stove to his right. Margerite's concern was making him uneasy.

"Irmgard told me," Margerite said, leaning back away from Carl, one hand on the seashell necklace she wore, "Herr Runge was a musician -- he played cello for the Bamberg Symphony. When he retired, they bought this Gasthaus."

Carl nodded, remembering the picture of the soldier, who must be their son.

"You don't look well, Carl," Margerite said with concern now. "Your face is so -- pinched."

"Yeah," he said, "I'm beginning to get light-headed a little. I don't feel so hot."

"If you think it is serious, Carl, you should go back to camp," Margerite said looking at his face closely.

"I don't know," he said, "but I think I better go to Sick Call at the dispensary -- and get check out one of these days -- soon."

He wiped his forehead with his hand and felt moisture.

Just as Carl was going to ask Sergeant Bowman how long they were going to stay out of camp tonight, Frau Runge came to the table with two large platters. One was stacked with two dozen fried eggs, the other with steaming fried ham pieces.

"I feel like an elephant is sitting on me," Carl said to the Sergeant, "and my cognac keeps coming up."

"If you're feeling crummy -- go lie down for a while -- sleep it off," the Sergeant said spearing a large piece of ham.

Then smiling he added, sliding an egg onto his plate, "I'm in no hurry to go home -- to face my wife. She's pissed at me. Ask the manager lady to give you a room -- I'll pay her. I'll pay for everything tonight," he said reaching for his cognac snifter. "Hell -- it's Fasching Night."

"Go," Rudi said. "That leaves more for us," waivin his arm, grinning widely, looking at the Sergeant for approval.

"Go Carl," Margerite said, "you can't enjoy -- if you don't feel well. Drinking more cognac will do no good," she said putting her hand on his arm, "that is for sure."

Carl followed Frau Runge to a room where there were three beds, a large one in the center of the room and smaller ones, each in an alcove with a window.

When the Frau left, closing the door, Carl slipped off his Eisenhower jacket and shoes, and stretched out on the bed near the door.

"Whew," he said, pulling up the blanket, "it feels tight inside my chest -- right in the center -- it's pushing out all my energy. I can't even hold my head up, hardly."

He had been asleep for more than a half-hour, when the door creaked, opening slowly. Light from the hall came over the bed.

"Carl," Margerite asked, "is everything all right?"

"Yes," he said squinting in the light, "I'm okay."

She swung the door closed; there was only the faint light coming from the parking circle below, outside.

"I came to see if you need help," she said coming to the bed. "I am not sure if you are sick -- or tipsy."

"Maybe a little of both," Carl said. "I've been feeling tired for better than a month or so, and lately -- I don't know -- I can't shake it off -- get rid of it."

"You should go to the doctor at the camp," she said in her crisp tone, "it could be serious."

Her concern for him made him feel he was special, as if she had singled him out of all the soldiers at the camp.

He reached up, and taking her arm, moved her down on the bed.

When he kissed her, she moved to lie down next to him.

"What are the others doing?" he whispered to the side of her face, sliding his hands up under her sweater.

"They are eating," she said, her hair brushing Carl's face as her skirt was pushed down, and she put a hand on his chest.

"No, no" she said, "let me do the work. You lie there," she climbed astride him. "Keep your strength."

Carl lay holding her buttocks as she raised and pushed against him, pumping in a motion that grew more intense. Her breasts flew up with each thrust, then dropped.

"Hold -- hold -- please -- hold."

Carl could feel inside her as if something suddenly contracted, then dropped, and she lay on him, her face moist against his.

She was spent, breathing heavy.

"That -- was wonderful," she whispered, breathless.

"More," he whispered back.

He was surprised how completely giving she was; she always acted so reserved. He was attracted to her pale blond hair, and detached mannerisms, that he knew now was an act -- probably to get along in the business world.

He enjoyed her white body, that was firm, like a sleek animal.

Sliding off to his side, she whispered, "No more, liebling -- we must not be seen."

"Once more," he said, raising up on one elbow, helping her out with her skirt, pleading, but knowing the answer was no.

"We must not be seen by the others," she said pulling on her sweater.

He reached to touch her hanging breasts, for a moment, before she pulled the sweater down.

She put her hand on the side of his face, just as the bedroom door swung open, light flooding over the bed.

Sergeant Bowman stood in the light.

"Margerite?" he said. "You in here?"

"Yes," she said getting to her feet. "I was just -- seeing if Carl was all right."

"You have your own room," Bowman said, unbuttoning his suit coat. "You," he said to Margerite slowly, as if holding back his drunkenness, "and Irmgard -- are bunking in another room -- down the hall. We got to -- act respectable -- here. You -- understand?"

"Thanks for checking on me," Carl said as Margerite went to the door. "I don't know what hit me like that. See you later."

She went out the door without speaking.

Bowman walked over to the large bed, and turning on the small lamp on the table next to it, said, "Phew -- I'm really in hot water at home with my wife -- but it's Fasching.

"I'll tell her we were partying -- all night," he said going over and closing the bedroom door.

Bowman hung his suit coat on the back of a chair, and when he was taking off his shoes, sitting on the bed, Carl asked, "Hey, where's Rudi?"

"He's with the women in the kitchen -- the Frau -- and Irmgard are cleaning up -- and he's still celebrating Fasching. He'll be up here -- later," Bowman said, snapping off the bed lamp.

Carl lay in the dark, wondering why Bowman brought Irmgard along for the party tonight -- if he was going to leave her down in the kitchen.

*   *   *   *   *

In the morning, Rudi came into the bedroom and pulled Carl's foot.

"We are all downstairs for coffee," he said. "Sergeant Bowman says we soon will go back to camp -- and I should wake you."

"Okay," Carl said blinking. When he put his feet over the side of the bed, he could still taste the sour that had come last night.

He made a winced face, saying, "Yeah, we don't want to pay for -- an extra day for -- sleeping too long."

"We are eating Belgian Waffles downstairs," Rudi said, grinning, "with honey." When he walked over to the door, he said without looking back, "We hope you are better today -- everyone is concerned."

"I feel better," Carl said pulling on a shoe, "but my mouth -- tastes like the bottom of an ashtray."

"Coffee is good for that," Rudi said, in the tone of one soldier talking to another, from the doorway, before he went out.

Downstairs in the kitchen, Carl sat down in the chair next to Margerite.

She stopped eating her waffle, looking at his face close.

"Are you better today?" she asked. "You are not so pale."

"I had a wonderful night," he said, but stopped while Irmgard came to pour coffee in his cup. When she moved away, he said to Margerite, "I want to continue -- where we left off last night."

"Hey, Carl," Bowman said, "you want to sweeten your coffee?" He was tilting the giant bottle, now about a quarter full, pouring cognac into his cup.

"No," Margerite said to Carl in a schoolteacher tone, "you should go to a doctor today -- and you should not go with alcohol on your breath."

Carl looked at her for a moment, then said to Bowman, "I'll skip the cognac -- I'm going on Sick Call when we get back to camp."

"You only live once," Bowman said holding up his cup. "Suit yourself, Carl."

Frau Runge came up behind Carl, offering a waffle from the platter she held, but he said, "No, just coffee," and suddenly felt nausea the food odor brought.

Not knowing what to do for his stomach, he picked up the coffee cup, and at first sipped some, then drank down the entire cup. The warmth gave him relief.

Leaning toward Margerite eating her waffle, Carl felt good enough to say quietly, "After I come from the doctor -- can I see you -- later today?"

"Not today," she said wiping the side of her mouth with a napkin. "I have a jewelry shipment coming up from Munich -- I must be at the Bahnhof -- and I must pay for my future shipment to come."

"Boy," Carl said, abrupt, "you're all business."

When his cup was filled, he picked it up quickly, and drank the coffee down without stopping.

Margerite was watching.

"Don't be silly, Carl," she said quietly. "You must go to the doctor -- you may have something serious wrong. Your health -- is very important."

Carl looked at her a moment, then nodded.

CHAPTER 8

Carl walked into the G-3 office at Regimental Headquarters, and slowly pulled off his overcoat.

"Cold, huh?" Flannery said from his desk. He had been typing and stopped.

"Yeah," Carl said hanging the olive-drab coat on a wall rack. "It goes right through your clothes -- it seems. I can never get warm."

"What the doctor say at the Dispensary?" Flannery asked, raising both arms to rest his hands on the back of his head.

"Well," Carl said sitting down at his desk, "he gave me three APC tablets -- and said I should drink a lot of water."

"That's it?" Flannery said lowering his arms.

"Yeah, and he said I should not make a habit of coming to the infirmary -- I could be charged with -- malingering."

"No, shit, Carl. Why'd he say that?"

"I asked if I could have an x-ray," Carl said. "I requested an x-ray of my chest."

"And he refused you?"

"He said he heard that in the German army, the doctors made sick-call complainers -- duck their heads in a bucket of cold water -- before leaving."

"That's crazy," Flannery said, leaning forward on his typewriter. "What you going to do now?"

"I'll come up with something," Carl said, and pulling open his desk drawer, and taking out a small bottle of cognac, quickly poured some into the coffee cup on his desk, then put the bottle back.

"Where's the major," he asked before sipping from the cup.

"They're all in an officer's conference with the Colonel," Flannery said, sitting up straight in his chair. "I think they're hashing over -- how to move the Regiment down to Grafenwhore next month."

"Yeah, I hear we're going for six weeks," Carl said sipping cognac. "Damn -- Field Training Exercises in the snow. That ought to be -- fun and games for everyone."

"Heh," Flannery grinned, "it'll sure put an end to your night adventures in Bamberg -- with that crowd from the Club."

"Quiet, Flannery."

It was better not to talk about the ride out the gate in Sergeant Bowman's Chevy -- it could lead to a full-blown Court Martial if the other Sergeants heard.

Carl was feeling light- headed from the cognac.

Smiling, he said, "It's kind of like Pleasure Island" to the room -- not talking to Flannery.

"Pleasure Island?" Flannery laughed. "What are you talking about, Carl? You better lay off cognac -- there's codeine in those APC tablets the doctor gave you --"

"Pleasure Island in the Pinocchio story," Carl said waiving an arm. "Everybody knows that."

"Pinocchio is a kid's story," Flannery said quietly. "What the hell -- has that got to do with anything?"

"Don't you remember all the bad boys in the story -- going off to Pleasure Island? There they smoke cigars, shoot pool, drink beer, -- even get to throw bricks through windows -- do anything they want," Carl said.

"Okay," Flannery said, "but I don't get it -- what you're leading up to."

"You don't get it -- the price they pay?" Carl said. "They turn into donkeys for all their mischief and are sold to work -- pull carts in the mines."

"I remember Pinocchio having a tail and donkey ears -- but I don't remember him turning into a complete donkey," Flannery said looking out the window, squinting.

"You're right," Carl said, sliding open the desk drawer with the cognac bottle, "he didn't turn completely into a donkey -- just partly."

"Carl," Flannery said in a hoarse whisper, "lay off that -- during duty hours -- that's real trouble if you get caught."

"Don't you get what I'm saying, Flannery?" Carl took a quick sip from the bottle, and put it back in the drawer, pushing it closed with both hands, while he thought.

"The Bowman Chevy ride out the camp gate is my ride to Pleasure Island -- Bamberg at night after the Club closes."

"Okay, Carl," Flannery said leaning forward over his typewriter, "I get that part."

"And Bowman pays my drink tab at the Club -- and he pays everything for everybody out on the town."

"Okay," Flannery said like a question.

"Why?" Carl asked. "Why does he do all that stuff?"

"Ah-h," Flannery said, "you think -- he's doing it to get you in trouble -- that he's setting you up?"

"Yeah," Carl said leaning back in his chair, hands on the desk. "What else could it be? He's working to have me Court Martialed -- to end up in the Stockade down in Mannheim."

"Why you think that?" Flannery said, leaning now with his elbows on his typewriter, "what reason has Bowman got for wanting to put you in Mannheim?"

"That's what I got to find out," Carl said quietly. "Why -- or for who -- Bowman is doing this stuff. I know he wears a Masonic ring -- if that means anything."

"This is serious, Carl," Flannery said getting up behind his desk. "Give me a snort of your cognac. This is like -- trying to solve a crime -- before it happens."

When the door of the Colonel's office opened, and the major followed by four other officers came out, talking, Flannery sat back down at his desk.

Carl slipped paper into his typewriter and began typing rapidly. He continued watching the officers talking, until the major went into his office, and the others left the room.

Flannery was typing a form paper, pretending, like Carl to be working. Carl was writing a letter home.

When he began to feel fatigued, Carl ducked down under the desk and sipped cognac; as he stood up, stretching for an instant, the major came out with a handful of papers, and went to Flannery's desk. He carried his overcoat on his arm.

"Type these as soon as you can," he said to Flannery, "and put them on my desk. I have to go out to a meeting now."

"Yes, sir," Flannery said, watching the major go out the door.

"Hey, Carl," he said, "can I have a sip of cognac? I need it for some reason today."

"Help yourself," Carl said, standing up and walking to the window. Looking out at the overcast sky, he added, "I'm feeling like shit."

He could hardly wait until quitting time, to get to the Club, and later out to Bamberg for a night of drinking.

It was easy to question why Sergeant Bowman was always paying for drinks, but it was hard to stop partying when the chance was offered. It was <u>impossible</u>, Carl thought, to stop.

*   *   *   *   *

The riot began in the Red Lion café, when a soldier suddenly stood up and threw a wine bottle at the orchestra stand. The music had been dull, workman like.

After the bottle smashed on the wall, the orchestra players ducking down, other soldiers jumped to their feet, throwing beer and wine bottles in every direction.

"What is this?" Sergeant Bowman said getting up from the table. "This is crazy."

"We should go," Margerite said pulling on her fur coat. "The police will come -- to arrest everyone."

A girl from the Club, a new waitress, out with Sergeant Bowman tonight, said, "There is a side door -- over there."

Margerite was reaching for her large purse on the floor, as Rudi pulled at Carl's arm, shouting, "The Military Police will be coming too -- come Carl."

"To hell with the MPs," Carl said, leaning out of his chair as Rudi pulled his arm. "I ain't afraid of -- no MP."

"Come," Margerite shouted, "while there is still time." She pulled Carl's other arm, helping Rudi lead Carl out. "You should not be foolish with the police," she shouted.

Sergeant Bowman and the waitress, holding hands, lead the way past the side of the bandstand, where the musicians were crouching down, protecting their instruments with arms.

Outside, a police siren was coming closer.

Margerite slid across the back seat of Bowman's Chevy, and pulling Carl's arm, shouted, "Get in -- quickly."

Carl stood up erect, looking over the top of the car, "I want to see what's going to happen -- when the cops show up," he shouted.

He took hold of the edge of the car roof with his free hand, Margerite pulling his other arm.

"No," Rudi shouted over the noise of the police siren, the car just up the street, coming, "no time for that." He pushed hard on Carl's back, making him fall into the car.

Sergeant Bowman and the waitress were watching Carl from the front seat. "Let's go," Bowman shouted; he had the car started.

Carl was still clinging to the car roof with one hand, when Rudi pushed him to get him fully in the back seat, and slammed the door.

"Yee-how," Carl screamed. "My hand is in the door."

Rudi pushed Carl again, after opening the door that did not close, and Carl fell across the seat, lying on Margerite's lap, his head hitting the window on her side of the car.

"Damn," Carl shouted, holding his hand. "Dammit -- I think some fingers are broken. The last two -- my right hand."

The flashing lights of the police car stopped ahead up the street; everyone in Bowman's car watching through the windows, as four policemen jumped out and ran into the café.

Bowman, driving away, slow in the opposite direction up the narrow street, said, "Okay -- where should we go?"

"I need a stiff drink bad," Carl said, holding his hand, sitting between Margerite and Rudi.

"Hey," Rudi said, "we can go to my apartment -- it's up the street here -- one street over. My wife works until two. I bought cognac for Fasching -- I did not open it yet. But we should be quiet -- not wake my son."

"My hand is going numb," Carl said. "Maybe I should see a doctor."

"How old is your son?" Margerite asked, interested. "I have a daughter in Munich -- she just turned four."

"He's three," Rudi said. "His name is Alexander."

"Some cognac," Bowman said to Carl, "will take the sting out of that hand -- at least until you go to the camp dispensary."

He had turned his head to talk, while driving.

"Okay," Carl said, "but let's make it fast -- the sting sort of sobered me up."

"Turn left here," Rudi said to Bowman, who turned the car slowly onto the narrow cobblestone street, "I live just there -- above that Boot maker shop -- there."

"We will get you a cognac," Margerite said quietly to Carl, a consoling tone in her voice, putting her hand on his wrist. "You will hurt less in a minute."

"The last two knuckles are flat," Carl said, appreciating the attention from her. "They're squashed, I think," he said rubbing the hand slowly. "They sting like hell."

"We will put ice on the hand," Margerite said, patting the wrist, "that will lower the pain."

"I hope so," Carl said. "I was dumb -- grabbing the car roof like that."

Going up the steps to Rudi's apartment, Bowman said, "It was smart ducking out of that riot -- those German cops and the MPs will bust a lot of heads -- before they arrest everybody."

"We must be quiet now," Rudi said unlocking the door. "Speak quiet -- we should not wake Alexander."

"Right," Carl said, holding Margerite, feeling her press against him as they stepped through the doorway.

Inside the apartment, they sat down on the couch, after slipping off their overcoats.

Rudi went into the kitchen, and came back with an ice cube tray, a towel over his arm, and a liter bottle of cognac.

"There are glasses on the table there," he said to Bowman, while setting the towel and ice cube tray on the couch arm, next to Margerite.

She put ice in the towel and wrapped Carl's hand; in the light he saw swelling all the way up the wrist.

Watching Rudi pouring cognac, Carl was impressed how everyone was being quiet. When he was handed a drink, Carl drank it quickly, holding out the glass for a refill.

Sergeant Bowman was standing with the new waitress over at the window, talking; holding their glasses of cognac, looking down at the street. Their foreheads were suddenly touching.

It was odd, Carl thought, the Sergeant never made a pass at Margerite, his age being close to hers in experience. He always seemed to have a different girl as a buffer, sort of.

There was a commotion at the door, and Carl saw Rudi's wife come in, home from her job at the café.

When she slipped off her coat, her full breasts showed in the low-cut blouse. She had the look of being totally vulnerable.

Rudi kissed the side of her face, and handed her a glass of cognac, speaking to her quietly.

"I want to look at Alexander first," she said, setting the glass down on a lamp table, on the way to the hallway, smiling to everyone.

Carl could not take his eyes off her. Standing up, holding his hurting hand, he said, "Can I use the bathroom?"

Rudi, pointing, "It's at the end, there in the hall."

Before Carl could make a move, Sergeant Bowman had stepped over to him, and holding his arm, whispered, "Don't go near Rudi's wife. She's off limits."

"I got to go piss," Carl said flatly, looking at Bowman. Then he unwrapped the ice pack towel off his hand, and dropped it on the couch. "And I want to look close at my hand -- in the light."

"Okay, okay," Bowman said, stepping back, taking a quick sip from his glass. "You know what I mean, Carl."

Walking in the hallway, Carl said to himself, "He's san odd duck." Shaking his painful hand, he mumbled, "He's sure not one to talk about -- how to act with women."

In the bathroom light, Carl, looking at the pale blue fingers, said, "That damn Rudi owes me -- for slamming that car door on my hand. But what can I do? I don't want to mess up everything."

Coming back out of the hallway, Carl saw Bowman kissing the new waitress over by the window.

Sitting down on the couch again, while he was wrapping the ice towel on his hand, Margerite slid her hand on his shoulder.

"I'm getting tired," he said to her quietly. "I want to go back to camp -- hit the sack. I've had enough for one night."

"I should go too," she said sliding her hand around his shoulders. "We'll get a taxi. I have early business tomorrow."

He took a sip of cognac, then finished the glass, standing up and walking to the window.

"Sarge, I got to head back to camp," Carl said evenly. "I'm really whacked-out tonight -- got to hit the sack."

"Can't you wait a while?" Bowman said, sounding half concerned. "I know your hand is bad, but what about the gate? The car is easier to pass the gate."

"I know," Carl pressed now saying, "but I'm getting loopy, can't keep my head up. I'm all in."

"Suit yourself, Carl," Bowman said, disinterested, looking back at the waitress, his arm around her waist.

Margerite helped Carl slide the sleeve of his overcoat over his sore hand.

"Thanks for the ice," Carl said to Rudi, as he watched Margerite taking the ice and towel to the sink out in the kitchen. "It helped take away the sting."

"Why are you going?" Rudi asked, helping Margerite, when she began pulling on her fur coat. "We have -- plenty of cognac."

"I know, I know," Carl said, buttoning his coat with his good hand, "but I'm just out of it tonight. I just feel too tired tonight."

"I wish you would stay," Rudi said to Margerite. "The party is just starting."

"I have business tomorrow," she said. "It is important -- I must get up early."

"It is <u>Fasching</u>," Rudi said disappointed. "And you two are leaving us -- I don't understand."

Outside, a heavy mist hung in the air, making the night seem to Carl, more cold. It penetrated through his overcoat, and he pulled up the collar with his good hand, then dropped it around Margerite's shoulders.

He felt her move against his side as they walked.

"Can we go to your hotel?" he asked quietly to the side of her face. "I want to make love -- before I go to camp."

"I am sorry, no," she said. "My room is at the Bahnhof Hotel -- it is no place for us to go. There are businessmen from Munchen using the train for coming and going. It would be bad for my business -- if they see me with a GI at the hotel."

Across the street from where they were walking, was a wide dark space with trees.

"What is that over there?" Carl asked slowly.

"A park," Margerite said. "There is a bridge there that goes over the river."

"What river?"

"The Bug," she said, pronouncing the name in German, 'Bo-og.'"

"I didn't know there was a river in Bamberg," Carl said looking, trying to see in the dark.

"It is very narrow," Margerite said smiling, walking in her long stride, looking up at Carl.

Her whole manner, Carl thought, was evidence her past was a privileged one. And the way she moved and spoke, and her knowledge of most things, was a sure clue she was educated.

She never spoke of her past, Carl thought, all the time we have been together. He told himself he had to wait for the right time and she would tell everything. Everybody was like that.

"Let's go over to the bridge," he said, sliding his good hand inside her fur coat, feeling her hip.

"What about the taxi?" she said. "And you said you were exhausted -- wanted to sleep."

"That can wait."

"How is the hand?"

"I looked at it," he said, putting his hand on her breast, "and two knuckles are about an inch higher than they should be -- up toward the wrist."

He kissed her, and when her coat fell open, he put his arm around the back of her waist, pulling.

Without talking, they began walking across the street to the park, their arms around one another.

"Oh," he said, "I see the bridge now, over there."

A mist rose from the narrow river that was more a stream than river.

They walked out to the middle of the wood plank bridge that was almost hidden by mist, and Carl kissed her, pushing his tongue between her lips, running his hand under her sweater.

She was silent and breathing heavy, when Carl lifted her to sit on the railing, pushing her legs apart, moving her wool skirt up. She stopped his hand.

She was doing something under her skirt for a moment, when Carl saw a soldier and short blond girl appear out of the mist at the end of the bridge.

As soon as the soldier saw their positions, he turned the blond around, holding her shoulders, and disappeared.

Whatever clothing Margerite removed, she slid into the pocket of her fur coat.

They were clinging to one another closely, Margerite's fur coat covering Carl's pushing against her, thrusting her sometime rising up, the sides of their faces touching.

"Um-m," she moaned suddenly, and she opened her mouth, looking up, gasping only, "Ah-h-h," quietly. "Ah-h."

She was silent when Carl kissed her, then helping get her skirt down.

A man in a light tan raincoat, hands in his pockets, came near the bridge on the walking path, but he kept his head down, and walking quickly, faded into the darkness.

"Damn," Carl said, "this is like making love in a train station." Then flipping his injured hand, he said, "It's beginning to sting like hell."

He made a face like he was blowing out a candle.

"Carl," Margerite said in a detached tone, "you must go to the barracks."

He was stunned for a moment; her cool manner and few words made him uneasy.

"Yeah," he said, "You're right. The numbness is wearing off."

She stood looking at his face, her hands in the fur coat pockets, pulling it tight around herself.

"Please, Carl, go now."

"Okay," he said. "Can I borrow a few Marks? I need money for the taxi -- we can drop you at your hotel, and I'll go to camp."

"Yes," she said, lifting her large purse off the wood planking of the bridge by the shoulder strap.

While her head was down, looking for coins in the purse, Carl wanted her more than ever before.

* * * * *

Carl asked the taxi driver to stop, when they were almost to Werner Cascerne gate, about a hundred feet short, where the lighting ended from the guard house and entrance gate.

He handed the driver the money and stepped out of the taxi quickly, running to the wall.

The gate guard saw him and came out, shouting, "Halt, you! Stop right there."

It was awkward for Carl climbing with his left hand and wearing an overcoat, trying to get his leg up to pull himself over the top of the wall.

He fell back.

"Halt," the guard said running along the wall toward Carl, but slowing when he saw him having difficulty.

Trying a second time, Carl could not get his weight up on the wall, falling back to the ground.

"Hey, stop," the guard said coming closer.

"I can't get up there," Carl said, and had to laugh.

"Get over," the SP guard said, "or I got to take you to the Guard house, buddy."

"I broke my hand in a fight," Carl said calmly, holding up the hurt hand, as the guard came closer.

Smiling, he asked the guard, "Can you give me a boost?"

The guard looked back toward the lighted gate for a moment, then cupped his hands. Carl put his foot up in the hands, and was boosted over the wall.

Neither of them spoke.

CHAPTER 9

"Looks as if the dissolute life is catching up with you," Private Copeland said to Carl sitting at the table in the PX cafeteria.

Carl smiled hearing the Harvard accent; he had been reading the <u>Stars and Stripes</u> newspaper, and had not noticed Copeland walking over.

"It's not as bad as it looks," Carl said lowering the newspaper, then, pulling at the bandage the doctor at the Dispensary put on that covered his hand and wrist. "Best yet, I'm scheduled for the bus that goes to the Army Hospital in Nuremberg today."

Copeland, smiling, set his coffee cup on the table.

"Were you in that brawl in town last night?" he asked sitting down across the table from Carl.

"Naw," Carl said, "it wasn't the riot, it was someone closing a door when I was looking in the wrong direction. My hand got caught in the door jam."

"That's what you told them at the dispensary?" Copeland asked grinning. "And you think they believed you?"

"Yep," Carl said confidently.

"I'm <u>sure</u> they believed you," Copeland said teasing, picking up his cup and sipping coffee.

"It's what happened. Believe it or not."

"If you insist, Breckles."

Holding the hand up at eye-level, Carl said, "The doctor at the dispensary said the hospital will x-ray it, and probably put on a cast."

Nodding, Copeland asked, "When are you leaving?"

His mood had changed from baiting Carl about the hand, to a more serious demeanor.

"At ten," Carl said looking at the bandaged hand, moving the fingers that were not covered, that were a dark blue. "It gets to Nuremberg at noon."

"Be careful what you say in Nuremberg," Copeland said leaning forward over the table. "You don't want them to get the impression you did it on purpose."

"Yeah," Carl said; he had been sipping coffee, and set the cup down. "I figured that subject would come up -- the regiment moving to Grafenwhore for training and all."

"You don't want them to get the impression," Copeland quipped, "sleeping on a folding cot for six weeks is not to your liking -- and you did something drastic."

"I know, I know," Carl said, "that's already been covered between me and the First Sergeant. I'm to report to Grafenwhore training area when I get back from the hospital. There's no problem there."

Leaning back in his chair Copeland asked, "How are you going to type with that hand?"

"I guess they'll have me answering the telephone a lot," Carl said quietly.

"Hey, where is our usual crowd of coffee drinkers? Our table is empty this morning," he asked to change the subject.

"They're probably packing for Grafenwhore," Copeland said, smiling. "On my way here, I saw the clerks loading the file cabinets from Personnel on trucks. Everything is going to Grafenwhore."

"Well, I got to go too," Carl said, sliding his chair back and standing. "I've got to change into my Class A uniform -- get my shaving stuff."

"I don't want to miss the bus."

"Good luck in Nuremberg, Carl."

"Thanks."

Crossing the cobblestone roadway to his barracks, Carl saw the Company Clerk from Fox Company on the steps to Regimental Headquarters. He carried a folder.

"Your friend Lasslett is in hot water again," the clerk shouted to Carl.

Stopping, Carl walked over to the steps to talk to Johnston, who he knew from sometimes helping with typing at the Regimental Headquarters office.

"What is it now?" Carl said, keeping his bandaged hand at his side.

"He disobeyed a Direct Order," Johnston said pushing up his eyeglasses. "The First Sergeant ordered him to pack his stuff for Grafenwhore -- get ready for the trucks. And he flat said, 'no.'"

"How come he did that?"

"He said his baby is sick -- at the apartment in Bamberg. He said he was going to leave camp and go to town to be with his wife and kid."

"Ah-h," Carl said. "That poor bastard."

"Sarge said he was told back in the States -- not to bring his wife and kid to Germany."

"Sort of late for that," Carl said raising his injured hand, holding it with his good hand, "the wife and kid are already here."

"He wants to talk to you. He asked me to tell you -- he's being held in the Company store room again."

"I can't go now -- I got to catch the hospital bus to Nuremberg," Carl said, feeling the excuse inadequate, due to Lasslett's serious situation. He knew Lasslett wanted help.

"They're going to throw the book at him," Johnston said, looking up the steps at the door to Headquarters, "because of all the trouble he made before."

Carl, looking at his wristwatch, said, "I better go talk to him. I've got about forty minutes before the bus leaves."

Carl went upstairs quickly to his barracks and changed to his dress uniform, and taking the pouch with all his toilet articles out of his locker, hurried back downstairs.

At Fox Company barracks, the First Sergeant swung open the door of the storage room, and Carl saw Lasslett was handcuffed to the iron bedframe.

"You did it again, huh?" Carl said, walking into the room, carrying his toiletries pouch in his good hand.

"I knew you'd show up," Lasslett said, sitting up, his handcuffed hand hanging close to the bedstead. "Sit down on the footlocker. I heard all about your hand, and the car door trouble."

"Right now," Carl said sitting down, "I only got a few minutes -- about twenty minutes till the bus leaves for the hospital in Nuremberg. I can't stay, you get it?"

"Carl, I need your help bad -- this time," Lasslett said running his hand over his hair concerned. "The baby is sick -- coughing and choking. My wife is scared as hell."

"I know, I know," Carl said. "But there is only one thing you got to do right now -- pack your equipment for Grafenwhore -- like they ordered you to do."

"Jackie called on the phone in the orderly room here," Lasslett said, as if not hearing what Carl said. "I told her to take the baby to the hospital in Bamberg.

"She said she would take a taxi to the hospital -- I'm sure she must have. She says she's scared -- alone with the baby sick -- living in a foreign country."

"Get your stuff packed for the Grafenwhore truck," Carl said, getting up from sitting on the footlocker, "and later, we can work something out -- talk to the Army Chaplain. Maybe we can get you a Compassionate Leave from the Chaplain -- or something like that."

Lasslett, rattling the metal restraints locked on the bedstead, said, "They put these cuffs on me -- they think I'll make a run for Bamberg to help her."

Carl did not say anything; he was looking at his watch.

"I've got to go," he said. "Will you listen to me -- pack your stuff -- you don't want to get Court Martialed. That's all I can tell you right now."

"Jackie was crying on the phone," Lasslett said, looking up at Carl, his free hand on the back of his neck. "She's really desperate."

"The baby's at the hospital," Carl said, getting irritated and walking toward the door. "You can't do anything more than that now -- except pack your stuff -- so you don't get Court Martialed."

"If you don't -- you could be in the clink for months."

"Will <u>you</u> go see my wife?" Lasslett asked, sitting up straight. "I mean when you're done at the hospital in Nuremberg."

"Yeah," Carl said rapping on the door for the Sergeant to open it, "when I get back -- having this hand looked at."

"I'm asking you to help me now," Lasslett said, snapping.

Carl shook his head going out the door, saying, "I am."

"You're some friend," Carl heard Lasslett shout, before the Sergeant closed the door.

"That guy will never learn," the Sergeant said to Carl, locking the door.

The medical bus to Nuremberg was the same as a school bus, painted army olive drab.

Carl sat in the rear of the bus, away from the women and children, who stay up front near the driver. They were dependents of Sergeants and Officers, going to the hospital along with the soldiers in the rear, who had major health problems that could not be treated at the camp Dispensary.

Carl looked at the soldier across the aisle of the bus, with broken glasses, one eye bandaged. Another soldier next to Carl on the seat, who Carl spoke to briefly, said he had a liver disease -- Hepatitis.

Everyone settled down when the bus rolled out of Bamberg into the flat farm country, except for one child, who continued crying no matter what the mother did to stop it.

A feeling of guilt came over Carl, as he sat looking at the farms and countryside out the bus window; the Army had Lasslett this time. He was headed for prison at Mannheim. That was a certainty. Carl felt he should have done more to help Lasslett, but he walked away, it seemed.

He had a perfect alibi for not helping, going to the hospital for the hand. But now, to himself, he had to admit that was not a strong enough excuse.

He had to face the truth for himself; he was <u>afraid</u> to help Lasslett again. He knew the Army would soon enough come after him -- for helping Lasslett, who seemed to always be against their policies and regulations.

Looking at the country in the distance, where hillsides had patches cleared of trees, as neat as if there had never been trees growing there, he asked himself why he felt so obligated to help Lasslett out of trouble.

How many times did he need to help Lasslett and his wife, when there is trouble?

He recalled the Bible says you must forgive your brother seven times seventy, or something like that. But that was an answer for <u>forgiveness</u>, not about helping a friend in trouble.

Another deep fear came across his mind. He could not get over the suspicion that Sergeant Bowman was setting him up to be Court Martialed. The night trips in the car out of the barracks gate were a soldier's dream -- too good to be true.

Bowman's reason for having him around was fishy from the beginning, Carl thought, but he had overlooked it. The chance for free drinks was hard to pass up.

He had to ask himself, already knowing the answer, if he was being set-up for a Court Martial.

* * * * *

At the hospital, Carl sat on a stool next to a Gurney, holding his hand out flat, watching the doctor injecting Novocain with a short needle into the side.

When he finished the injection, the doctor picked up an x-ray of the hand from a side table, and looking at it closely, asked, "You fought?"

"No, sir," Carl said, looking at the doctor's Captain bars, his black hair combed back neatly, and his nametag saying: NAVARRE. "I had a car door slammed on my hand."

Showing no reaction, the doctor began pushing the knuckle caps down, from where they had been moved up by the impact of the door.

"Does this hurt?" he asked.

"Not much, sir," Carl said wincing.

When the knuckle joints were where the doctor wanted them, he said to Carl, "You will wear a plaster cast up to the wrist -- for a month."

The nurse, who had washed the hand in alcohol earlier, came back into the room, and the doctor said to her, "Fourth and fifth metacarpal -- a cast for thirty-days."

Carl watched her writing on a clipboard. She was a second Lieutenant with a plump face.

"I'll call the orderlies," she said to the doctor.

"Will I be able to use the hand in the cast?" Carl asked the doctor, who was washing his hands at the sink.

"If you are careful," the doctor said, his back to Carl. "It will be stiff after it heals -- you must do exercise therapy later."

He wiped his hands with a towel, dropped it into a hamper, and went out the door, without saying more.

After the cast was put on, the nurse led Carl back to the ward, and he lay out on the bed. To his surprise, he had been admitted to the hospital, given pajamas and assigned to a bed. At first he had protested, saying it was only the hand that was injured; he was not bed-sick.

The gruff orderly, who looked like a football linebacker, said, "Mac, when you're admitted, you go to bed."

He got a similar answer the second day of his confinement, when he asked the orderly if he could get a chest x-ray.

"My chest aches right in the center," he told the orderly, "and some mornings, I wake up wet with sweat."

"I thought, while I'm here in the hospital," he said calmly, "I could get a chest x-ray -- check it out."

"You aren't scheduled for no chest x-ray," the orderly said. "If you got chest trouble, you should report to your post dispensary. They can ask for an x-ray here." He walked away before Carl could ask anymore.

Four days later, the doctor came to Carl's ward on the morning rounds, and examined the cast carefully.

"Move the fingers as much as you can," the doctor said, turning the hand over to look at the underside. "Circulation is important to a hand in a cast. You could get gangrene. If you see the veins go black -- see a doctor immediately. You understand?"

"Yes, doctor," Carl said quietly. "There's one other thing, Sir. I'd like to get a chest x-ray."

"What's wrong with your chest?"

"Well, Sir, I have sharp pains in the center, sometimes," Carl said sheepishly. "And I feel like I have a cold, or some kind of congestion, that I can't shake off -- it won't go away."

"All right," the doctor said, "I will prescribe an x-ray." He was writing in a folder lying out on the bed, when he said, "If the cast begins to itch, pour mineral oil on the skin under the cast."

"Yes, doctor," Carl said. He was sitting up at the edge of the bed, holding the arm up for the doctor to examine. "Ah-h, Sir, when do you think I'll be going back to my unit in Bamberg?"

"Tomorrow," the doctor said, "but for certain -- the next day." Closing the folder, he added, "Be sure to watch those veins."

"Yes, Sir, I will. I don't want gangrene."

*   *   *   *   *

Carl missed taking an x-ray the next day when he boarded the medical bus back to Bamberg that left at nine that morning.

The Regiment moved to Grafenwhore two days before, taking all their equipment with them. The old major in G-3, who had stayed behind, gave Carl the job of answering the telephone in the Regimental Adjutant's office. He scribbled phone messages with his good hand, holding the telephone with the good fingers of the injured hand in the cast.

"Private Breckles," the old major said coming into the Adjutant's Office, "you stay and answer the phone until noon. My Jeep is leaving now -- taking me to Grafenwhore --"

"Yes, Sir," Carl said, interrupting the major, "but how am I going to get to Grafenwhore?"

"You will ride with Sergeant Mullenburger -- he has a car," the Major said, adjusting his glasses on his nose. "The Eighty-Seventh Regiment will replace ours here at camp for six weeks -- their trucks are showing up outside headquarters, just now."

"You answer the phone here until noon, get the last of our Regiment's messages. Then let the Eighty-Seventh people take over."

"I understand, Sir."

"Mullenburger should have all the maps the Regiment needs completed by noon," the Major said pulling on his jacket. "You two will be the last of our people to leave the camp."

"Yes, Sir," Carl said nodding, understanding now why Mullenburger was staying back.

He was a German Cartographer, who joined and trained with the American Army, and was sent back to Germany, and now was assigned to reproducing all sorts of maps in the basement of Regimental Headquarters.

It was almost noon when Carl came down the steps of Regimental Headquarters, dragging his heavy duffle bag.

He stood for a moment watching clerks from the visiting regiment, unloading file cabinets off a truck.

"We should go now," Mullenburger said, opening the trunk of his Mercedes parked near the basement door of headquarters.

He put both duffle bags in the trunk and slammed the lid.

"What's your first name?" Carl asked opening the front door of the car, seeing the back seat was stacked with maps up to the car ceiling. They were large maps, rolled up, looking like cordwood; they were very detailed maps, Carl found out later, with different shades of green for topography.

"My first name is Otto," Mullenburger said starting the car.

"Ah," Carl said, "a diesel," listening to the rattling engine.

Looking at the dashboard, Carl saw the car was utilitarian, not plush; the kind of Mercedes used for taxicabs in Germany.

"Yes, they are very economical to run," Otto said, a tinge of pride in his tone, as they drove toward the gate. "The large petrol -- gas companies have lobbyists to keep the diesel out of the U.S. Maybe they are too much economical."

Carl shrugged, not commenting on Otto's remark; he was looking up at the Enlisted Men's Club as they drove up to the gate guardhouse. It made him think of Margerite, who, last night had not showed up at the club. Maybe she was down in Munich, or maybe buying more shell jewelry in Yugoslavia on the Dalmatian Coast someplace, he told himself.

It did not matter, Carl thought, because the whole stinking regiment was down in Grafenwhore anyhow -- there was no business for her at the Club.

Otto nodded to the gate guard as they drove out of camp, and Carl waived, smiling.

"You know the roads to take to Grafenwhore?" Carl asked, still grinning. "If you don't -- we certainly got enough maps in the back seat."

"I know the way," Otto said in his assured manner, as he turned the car south toward the Autobahn expressway. "I grew up -- in a small village near Bayreuth."

CHAPTER 10

When Otto turned onto an overpass, the Autobahn below with speeding cars, Carl asked, "Hey, aren't you taking the 'Bahn?"

"I am not in a hurry for Grafenwhore," Otto said in blunt English. "Besides, the supply trucks from the regiment are not driving the Autobahn. They are on the roads ahead. I was asked to report on them for the G-3 Office."

Carl looked at Otto's face from the side; it was a peasant face, the chin out almost as far as the nose.

"Okay," Carl said, grinning, "maybe we can stop in some village Gasthaus -- have a drink of cognac."

"Yes," Otto said, "we will stop for a lunch."

Carl smiled, moving his fingers in the cast that lay on his thigh.

"I need a drink," Carl said slowly, "my hand aches."

"Your drinking," Otto said, "is going to get you in trouble -- like your friend Lasslett."

"Maybe so," Carl said quietly, looking at Otto again, wondering where that remark came from, and what he knew.

"I heard Lasslett was moved to Wurzburg three days ago," Otto said in a matter-of-fact manner, while turning onto a road that led up into rolling hills in the distance.

"Really?" Carl said in unbelief. "When I went to Fox Company -- after the hospital -- they didn't tell me he was in Wurzburg. They just said he had been 'moved.'"

"He is to be Court Martialed at Division Headquarters," Otto said without emotion.

"He's had the <u>Schnitzle</u> now," Carl said. "He'll be lucky if he gets off with six months in the Mannheim jail."

"I hear Lasslett has his wife living in Bamberg."

"Yeah," he does, Carl said looking out the window on his side of the car. He was not feeling well; a sharp pain in the center of his chest, draining his energy.

He looked out at the stream that ran near the road. The water was moving rapidly, despite patches of ice and snow lying across it.

"She is good-looking, I hear," Otto said grinning, "like a Barbie-Doll."

Carl smiled, "Yeah, a Barbie-Doll with black hair."

"If they put Lasslett in the Army prison," Otto said turning to look at Carl, "it will be hard for her -- for sure."

"She has a baby with her too," Carl said.

"She should go back to the States," Otto said, quickly.

A discrete sign appeared on the left side of the road: Bayreuth Festival. Behind the sign began a narrow dirt road, between two tall shrubs. Carl could see nothing up the road.

"What kind of festival is that?" Carl asked, knowing Otto was fishing for information about Lasslett's wife -- him being a close friend. The sign question was a ruse to change the subject.

"It's the Wagner festival -- it happens every year. They play all the Ring Cycle music. People come from all over the world to hear."

Otto spoke to Carl in a tone like an angry teacher.

"In the summer, they play Wagner operas -- and they call it a festival -- in the outdoors."

"I don't like operas much," Carl said, looking out at the stream again, remembering Hitler was an admirer of Wagner for the music he wrote about German Mythology.

Wagner's grandniece still lived on the property, Carl read in the newspaper once. She was a supporter of Hitler, back before the war the newspaper article also said.

"Ah-h," Otto said suddenly, "look there -- up ahead. Army trucks at the side of the road."

Carl saw only three trucks.

The lead truck had the hood up, and two soldiers were leaning working on the engine. Carl saw the last of the three trucks had the tailgate down, a wide tool chest showing, with rows of drawers.

"Hope they get that thing running," Carl said, sitting up straight from slumping in the seat, pulling his fatigue cap down closer over his eyes as they passed.

He had seen all the soldiers turning, looking at the Mercedes as it passed.

"Up ahead, must be the convoy," Otto said.

"Oh, yeah," Carl said looking up the road. "There they are -- there's a whole string of trucks on the side of the road.

"Is this as far as they got? They left camp early this morning?" Carl asked.

"They are not in a hurry to get to Grafenwhore," Otto said crisply.

As they approached the string of trucks, Carl saw the soldiers in field jackets, standing next to the trucks, some smoking. Some were standing in small groups.

An officer, a Lieutenant in starched fatigues, saluted as the Mercedes approached.

Carl, feeling sheepish, and unable to salute back, slid down in the seat. He could not return the salute with the cast on his hand.

The thought he did not belong here crossed his mind suddenly. This travelling in a Mercedes put everything out of perspective; he was only a private, and here he was riding like a general in a car with a load of maps on the back seat.

When the young Lieutenant saluted, it completed the illusion of what he *appeared* to be, and he felt uneasy.

"I probably look like General Rommel going to the front in this Mercedes," Carl said, lifting his cap off his eyes.

"No," Otto said quickly. "But maybe General Patton," he added, driving the Mercedes over to the road lane that was away from the trucks. He was grinning.

"Hurry up," Carl said. "The sooner we get past this convoy, the better."

* * * * *

It was snowing for the second day at Grafenwhore, the morning Carl woke up on the folding cot in the Regimental Headquarters' hut. His cot was next to the Adjutant's desk. He was to answer the phone in the event a snap alert from Headquarters Division was given for a training exercise.

He had dressed, and was dismantling the cot, when the Major came in the door, wearing a parka.

"Morning, Sir," he said, stacking the folded cot in the corner near the stove. "No alert call last night."

"You can go to the Mess Hall," the Major said while taking off his parka. "I'll take the phone calls now."

"Right, Sir," Carl said while setting his rolled sleeping bag on top the folded cot.

As he was slipping his right hand with the cast, through his field jacket sleeve, Carl was careful not to snag the rayon pile lining; he did not want to break the cast where it was thin, just over the last two fingers.

He had been moving the fingers, like the doctor told him, to keep the circulation moving.

There were three weeks to go, before he was to report back to the hospital in Nuremberg, and he was determined to get the hand back to normal.

After showering and shaving in his barracks hut, he walked down the row of huts to the Headquarters Company Mess Hall. All these huts were the same: oversize garages, cement floor, wood walls, and a small furnace.

Carl was sitting at a table eating scrambled eggs, when he saw Flannery come in the door.

"You hear about Lasslett?" Flannery asked, leaning on the edge of the table.

Carl shook his head with a mouthful of eggs.

"He got six months in prison at Mannheim -- and forfeiture of all pay and allowances," Flannery said quietly. "The guys in Fox Company just told me."

"That poor bastard," Carl said slow.

Flannery turned, and went to the coffee urn, and when he came back to sit at the table, said, "Lasslett's wife is going to be frantic. She's in a foreign country -- without him -- for six months, and without any money. Maybe she can turn to her folks in the States for help."

"Maybe not," Carl said, "Jackie ran away from home with Lasslett." Then as he put his fork down on his empty plate, slowly, he added, "They didn't want her to marry Lasslett -- in the first place."

"But now that she's in a jam," Flannery said, "they have to forgive and forget -- maybe send her air fare home."

"Carl, they can't just leave their daughter out in the cold."

"Yeah," Carl said, pushing away his food tray with his good hand, "I guess you're right about her folks -- they'll have to help Jackie."

"Maybe," Flannery said after sipping coffee, "you should check on her <u>now</u> -- you being a good friend of her husband -- she might do something crazy."

"How can I help?" Carl said sliding the tray further away on the table, "I'm stuck down here in Grafenwhore."

"Well, maybe when you get to go back to the hospital."

"Yeah, that's three weeks away."

"That's better than nothing," Flannery said holding the coffee cup with both hands. "You should do <u>something</u> -- you're his buddy."

"Okay, okay, I get the message," Carl said, picking up his coffee cup, wondering why Flannery was pushing so hard for him to go visit Lasslett's wife. "You're beginning to sound like <u>Father</u> Flannery."

"Well," he said smiling, "I did go to Saint John's in Brooklyn."

"I thought that was a basketball school," Carl said.

"That too," Flannery said with a straight face.

"I'll look her up," Carl said, "as soon as I can -- if she hasn't gone back to the States by the time I get there."

*   *   *   *   *

Two days later, Carl slipped in the morning, crossing the frozen walkway to the Headquarters hut, and broke the cast.

He had fallen once before, putting his hands out to brake the fall when he slipped, but this time he landed on the cast with all his weight.

When he saw the blue-black vein on the underside of his forearm, where the cast had broke and opened, he went on sick call that morning.

"I can't do anything about this here," the Medic at the Dispensary said, while examining the arm, "so we got to send you back to Bamberg."

"How am I going to get to Bamberg?" Carl asked concerned.

"The Mail truck goes to Bamberg every day," the Medic said, turning to a cabinet for a minute. "You can catch a ride -- I'll turn in the report -- so the paperwork will go with you."

Before Carl could stand up from the gurney, the Medic took hold of the arm, saying "Just a second, let me put disinfectant on that arm."

He poured what smelled like alcohol to Carl, through the crack onto the skin under the cast. The alcohol felt cold as it trickled down the arm as Carl watched, intently.

"The Mail truck leaves from the Post Office," the Medic said. "You better get over there -- I'll send the papers in the Daily Distribution envelope."

There was no room in the cab of the deuce-and-a-half Mail truck. The driver and his assistant sat up there.

"There's no heater up front, either," the driver said to Carl, looking at the assistant, who was reading a copy of "The Stars and Stripes" newspaper. "So we'll all be cold," the driver, with a face like a chipmunk said, "we'll <u>all</u> freeze."

Climbing up in back, under the canvas top, Carl stretched out on the pile of mailbags. He took off his wool scarf and wrapped the cast hand to keep it warm.

Back in Bamberg, Carl was told he was being sent to the Nuremberg Hospital for treatment, but the bus today had left; he would go tomorrow. He was not looking forward to riding with the 'dependents;' the wives and crying kids of officers and sergeants down in Grafenwhore.

Carl slept in the Education Building alone. He did not go downstairs to the Enlisted Men's Club; the arm had him worried. His concern now was to have it examined, and he avoided drinking in case there was infection, and he would need an anti-biotic in his system.

His chest had a sharp ache, off and on; it was not a dull ache, but sharp, like a pinch inside. He was convinced there was something very wrong in there, but he would wait, do what was needed, after the hand was all right.

Carl thought all this while dressing the morning he was scheduled to go on the bus to Nuremberg, putting on his wool Class A uniform with the Eisenhower jacket.

He put on his overcoat for extra warmth, and instead of going to the Mess Hall, full of the replacement troops who took over the Regimental buildings, he walked slowly to the PX cafeteria in the snow.

There were no familiar faces in the whole camp, he saw by walking, careful not to slip again, feeling out of place, as if he did not belong here any more. Bamberg was changed.

In the cafeteria, he was slow in cutting the French toast on his plate, with the fork in his left hand, when he glanced up and saw Jackie Lasslett standing at the cashier counter.

She was holding the baby in one arm.

Walking up to her, he said, "Jackie, hello. Come over to my table for a minute. We can talk."

She looked at him, startled; as if unbelieving it was him.

"Where have you been? Mike told me to find you," she said looking at him, shifting the baby to her other hip, "and nobody knew where you were."

"I'll explain," Carl said, quietly. "Come over to the table --"

"Let me pay for the baby food," she said. "I'll be right over."

Carl saw dark circles under her eyes.

She was not dressed in the Poodle skirt like at Fort Riley. She wore Levi's and a short jacket. Her Bouffant hairdo was gone, her black hair pulled back to a pony tail.

At the table, Carl ate the cold French toast, and watched Jackie coming across the floor; she walked slow, as if unsure of herself.

"I heard about Wurzberg, and the Court Martial giving Mike six months -- and the fine. But how is he doing?"

He watched Jackie set the bag of baby food on the table, saying, "I got a letter yesterday," then sit down.

She opened her coat, while holding the baby, "He's going on a hunger strike," her eyes filling with tears, she said slow, "until we can some see him.

"He's very worried about me and the baby."

"Yeah," Carl said looking at the baby, "he has to be desperate -- it's not hard to understand why."

Rocking the child, Jackie said, "And to make things worse, Martha here has a fever."

"Do you know what it is?" Carl said sipping the lukewarm coffee in his cup.

"I think she has an infected ear," Jackie said, looking at the child's head. "So we're going to the Nuremberg Hospital today -- to have her looked at by a pediatrician."

"Hey, I'm going to Nuremberg too," Carl said, leaning back in his chair. "The dispensary sent me back from Grafenwhore -- to go to the hospital. How's that for coincidence?"

"Great," Jackie said, biting her lower lip for a moment, "now there's somebody to talk to -- for a change."

Carl looked at the child, then said, "I hope it's nothing serious -- her ear."

"I had her checked at the hospital in Bamberg," Jackie said, "and they said the damp weather was causing flu-like trouble. I took her home -- I wanted to go to Mike's Court Martial. But when the Army moved it to Wurzburg, I couldn't go.

"Then Martha had a leaking out her right ear -- so I'm going to the Nuremberg hospital -- for an Army pediatrician to look at it."

Carl sat nodding, when Jackie asked calmly, "Why do you have a cast on your hand?"

"It's just a broken finger," he said holding it up. "I fell and broke the cast, so I'm going back to the hospital where they put it on."

"Does it hurt?"

"No," he said. He looked at the cast for a moment, then picked up his coffee cup, "this is cold -- I'm going for a warm-up. Can I get you a cup?"

"Yes -- great."

While she moved the child to her other arm, Carl, getting up, saw a stain on her blouse; it was a dry stain that had been there for a time.

Coming back to the table with a tray for the two cups, Carl said, "It's getting close to the time for the bus to leave."

"I'm ready," Jackie said, and he saw she was savoring the hot cup of coffee. "I've been so busy with Martha -- I haven't even done the laundry -- and on top of it -- I ran out of baby formula."

"Things go like that -- sometimes."

"I'm really worried about Mike," she said holding the cup with both hands in front of her face. "I mean -- I hope he doesn't do something drastic. I wish you could talk to him," she said looking over the cup. "He always listens to what you say. You could tell him not to do something foolish in prison -- and make things worse."

"All right, I'll see what I can do," Carl said looking up at the cafeteria clock. "It might come down to me writing a long letter of fatherly advice."

"I wish I could go to Mannheim to see him," she said, setting the cup down slowly into the saucer, "but with the baby sick -- it's too big a problem right now."

"We better get over to the Dispensary," Carl said softly, "the bus leaves at ten sharp."

She zipped her jacket closed, shifted the baby, then reached for the shopping bag.

Getting up, Carl said, "Hey, you aren't going to carry that shopping bag all the way to Nuremberg are you?"

"I can't run it home, there isn't time."

"Give it to me," Carl said reaching. "I'll set it under my desk in Headquarters."

"I don't want to -- lose it."

"Naw, it'll be there when you get back."

Outside, Carl walked up the steps at Regimental headquarters, hoping there was nobody familiar around. It would get back to Lasslett fast, his wife was excited by another soldier.

They were all unfamiliar faces in the G-3 Section when Carl went forward to his desk, not speaking, walking deliberately.

No one questioned him; the replacement clerks watching as he put the shopping bag in the desk well, but they did not speak, some continued their typing.

Jackie stood waiting at the bottom of the steps, holding the baby.

"When you get back," Carl said walking slow down the steps, his chest hurting from the exertion he had been through, "just walk in -- and pick up your bag. You don't have to say anything to the clerks."

They were walking to the Dispensary, when Jackie said, "Martha will get her noon feeding at the hospital."

Carl nodded, putting his hand on his chest where it hurt.

On the bus, Jackie took a seat half-way to the back of the bus, and with her holding the baby, Carl was suddenly aware, they appeared like a young military family. But it was not real.

He sat wondering why he was trapped into helping Lasslett and his family, and he did not know how to get out of it.

For relief, he looked outside the bus window, the road ran next to railroad tacks, monotonously, except for an occasional cluster of houses.

Then the bus passed around a farm wagon on the road, the wagon rolling on rubber car tires, the driver walking next to a load of turnips.

Jackie began talking about how expensive it was living on the German economy, the rent and food prices were high, and how she was thankful for the PX Commissary, and the low prices for American foods.

"You know what cheese most Germans prefer?" Carl asked, to keep the awkward conversation going.

"They have all kinds over here," Jackie said, looking down at the baby sleeping, she was holding with both arms.

"Velveeta," Carl said. "Of all the kinds of cheeses they have here in Europe -- Germans buy Velveeta the most."

"Maybe," Jackie said smiling, "they buy it -- because it's American."

"Maybe," Carl said grinning. "I read about the Velveeta bonanza in an article in the Stars and Stripes newspaper."

She did not react the way Carl had expected, the irony of Europeans liking a commercial cheese, and he felt admiration for her. She was not a Barbie-doll, and he was beginning to be drawn to her.

After a pause, Jackie said, It's not really the food and rent stuff that's the problem now -- it's Mike being away. It's hard to get used to."

Carl sat quietly, wondering if he could put his arm around her, and what she would do.

"He's only been gone a week," she said quietly, "and it's getting harder every day -- being alone all the time."

Carl was about to suggest she go home, back to the States for a few months, but changed his mind.

Instead, he said, "If you're short of money, I've got about a hundred and forty bucks in Soldier's Deposits -- you're welcome to it."

"No, no," Jackie said smiling, looking at him and shifting the baby, who was sleeping. "My mother back in Wisconsin sends me money every month -- but don't tell Michael."

Carl nodded, and turned away from looking at her face, glancing out the window of the bus.

"Ah," he said, partially to distract himself, "looks like we're coming into Nuremberg."

He felt better that this close-talk with Jackie was coming to an end. It was getting too personal. She was a woman who was married to a friend, he told himself, and you better remember that.

He deliberately did not look at her face again, up close.

*   *   *   *   *

In the hospital, the orderly who cut the cast off said to Carl the hand did not look like it healed properly, and the doctor might have to break and re-set the bones.

Carl began to sweat, thinking about breaking the fingers again, sitting with his hand on the table, covered with a towel. When the doctor came into the room, he immediately asked, "Does it hurt -- when you break the fingers?"

"Who said anything about breaking fingers?" the doctor asked, taking the towel away, looking close at the grey hand.

"I heard --"

"You heard wrong," the doctor said, turning the hand over to look at the underside of the arm.

He was a Major, gold leaves on his uniform collar, under the white clinic coat he wore.

"We're going to keep you here in the hospital for a few days," the doctor said, after checking the veins on both sides of the arm, setting the arm down on the table, gently.

"Then we'll put another cast on -- a smaller one, later, after we're sure there is no infection."

"Yes, Sir, thank you, Sir," Carl said as the doctor was writing in a folder, thanking him for the medical service, but more so for eliminating any bone breaking.

Three days later, the same morning he was to go back to Bamberg, Carl was given the chest x-ray he requested, and he asked the orderly putting on the new cast, when he could see the x-ray films.

"It'll be a day or two," the orderly said, "they're really busy in Radiology. It'll probably be sent to your Regiment's Dispensary," he said, working, his hands covered with white plaster.

"Check with your Dispensary when you get back."

Carl felt relieved from his medical problems for the time being, as he dressed for the bus trip back to Bamberg at noon. He had accomplished a lot in three days.

He wondered too, how Jackie did here at the hospital with the baby's ear, but mostly, he wondered about Jackie.

CHAPTER 11

A night training exercise was ordered the last weekend Carl's Regiment was at Grafenwhore.

It was near eleven at night, Carl was boiling water in the G-3 hut for the officers, who were visiting First Lieutenant Taylor, the Officer of the day on duty.

The coffee they were drinking came from packets in the C-ration cartons, a dry coffee powder emptied into hot water.

Outside in the dark, a "Long Tom" cannon would fire at intervals of about twenty minutes. The 250-millimeter cannon is the largest gun the army has, and in addition to regular cannon shells, it could fire shells with nuclear warheads.

The giant gun was always fired at night, so no one would see it in operation, especially the Soviet Bloc troops on winter maneuvers, just over the hills to the east in Czechoslovakia. But the Communist soldiers could hear the powerful cannon when it fired, an earth-shaking blast.

Carl poured hot water into the cups for the officers from Battalions in the Regiment, who had served with First Lieutenant Taylor in Korea, listening to their conversation.

They sat on folding chairs in front of Lt. Taylor, who sat behind a large folding table cluttered with maps, papers, and four telephones.

When the big cannon went off outside, the shock waves rattled the front door, making the maps on the wall flutter, and the floor vibrate.

"You think that cannon is really going to make a difference?" one Lieutenant asked the group at the table. He was stirring the powder coffee in the hot water of a canteen cup with a pencil from the table. "If the Russians come at us here in Germany -- it won't stop the attack. How can it make a difference?"

"The Fulda Gap," Lieutenant Taylor said, arms resting forward on the able, "is the only place Russian tanks can get through the mountains to the flat country of western Europe.

"The 'Long Tom' can blast anything that tries to get through the bottleneck -- the narrow gap. They won't get through the gap -- the tanks won't."

Carl, listening, walked back to the stove, and put more water in the pot to boil. He had never thought of being attacked here in Germany, and now he wondered what he would do if war came.

"Do you think they would ever use atomic shells -- in that monster gun?" a Lieutenant with "Becker" on his jacket nametag asked Lieutenant Taylor. He sat sideways in his chair, one arm draped over the back.

Carl knew the man in Item Company nick-named Becker, Lieutenant Lister Bag, after the bulgy, company-sized water bag that was hung from a shoulder-high tripod. He was portly with a round face, and easy to make jokes about.

"We have atomic shells in hidden ammo dumps," Lieutenant Taylor said calmly, "that are under twenty-four hour guard."

He sipped coffee from his tin canteen cup for a moment, then added, "If we need them, we'll use them."

A thin Second Lieutenant, who wore a parachute jump pin, said, "The Russians know we have these atomic shells -- to stop them -- don't they?"

"Uh-huh," Lieutenant Taylor said looking over at him, "that's why they started the Korean War."

"How's that?" Lieutenant Lister Bag asked, he was tearing open a foil packet of coffee, his cup between his knees.

Just then, the Long Tom fired and the room shook again.

"With our Army standing here in Europe -- eyeball-to-eyeball -- with the Russians," Taylor said, leaning on the table, "they were forced to look for a no-count place to start a war -- to break the tension -- take the heat off themselves."

"So that's why the Korean War started," the Lieutenant with the parachute jump badge said. "They wanted to tie-up the U.S. -- make us fight -- defend a place that didn't have much consequence."

"Yes," Taylor said, "they had the Communist North Korea invade the South Koreans, knowing the U.S. would defend the South -- it's a Democracy."

"That was back in nineteen-fifty," Lieutenant Lister Bag said, stirring his fresh-made coffee with a pencil, again.

Lieutenant Taylor was caught sipping coffee, and he nodded, but did not speak.

"Okay," the parachute Lieutenant said, "Korea broke the tension back then -- but here we are again in nineteen-fifty-five -- training to take on the Russians."

Carl watched the parachute Lieutenant get up from his chair and come over to the stove. Carl, listening intently, poured hot water into his cup.

"What happens now?" the parachute Lieutenant asked Taylor. "I mean what happen if a Russian tank gets through -- the Fulda pass?"

He sat down and picked up a packet of coffee off the table, sprinkling it into the steaming cup on the table.

"That's why we're here," Lieutenant Taylor said. "To try and stop them."

"<u>Try</u> is right," the parachute Lieutenant said, using Taylor's spoon on the table. "We might slow them up a little -- we're only a regiment, we can't stop an army."

"That's right," Lieutenant Taylor said folding his hands on the table, "the Army predicts we'll take ninety-nine percent casualties -- all of us down the drain -- even the cooks and clerks -- killed or captured."

"Jeeze," Carl said from his chair next to the stove, excited, "you mean we'll all be wiped out? That's the Army's plan for us?"

"Naw," Carl said, his face red, sheepish for his outburst, "the army will stop them -- from taking over all of Europe."

"They will probably have to stop the attack at the Rhine," Taylor said, just as the Long Tom fired. "The allies," he began as the shock wave passed, interrupting, "can bring up supplies across France, enough to make a stand against the Russians, from the other side of the Rhine."

"That is a real Doomsday scenario for us in the Army stationed here in Germany," Lieutenant Lister Bag said, looking at his watch. "But Doomsday or not -- it's time for me to make the rounds of the guard posts."

He was the first to stand up. The other Lieutenants drank, finishing their coffee quickly, and got up on their feet.

"Duty calls," the Parachute Lieutenant said walking to the hut door, the others following.

Carl, listening to all this visceral war-talk, began to ask himself if he should ask Lieutenant Taylor about what he should do about his chest ache problem; he had the feeling his energy was dropping lower each day.

He knew instinctively he was sick, something wrong in his chest, but he could not prove it. The Dispensary was no help -- in fact they seem to be fighting him.

What triggered the thought in Carl, was Lieutenant Taylor saying "ninety-nine percent casualties" if the Regiment was attacked by the Russians. For some reason, the fatal sound of the statement made Carl feel he was vulnerable.

Carl, like the others who came to talk with Taylor, had a feeling of reassurance when the Lieutenant spoke. His knowledge of things gave the listeners a confidence in his leadership. People looked up to Taylor and would do what he asked. Follow him. He was someone to trust in time of crisis.

Hesitating, Carl was fighting to decide if he should ask Lieutenant Taylor what to do about his chest problem.

Remembering with a smile, Carl thought of the photograph he had seen in Lieutenant Taylor's desk drawer, back in Bamberg Headquarters. The photo showed Taylor on graduation from Texas A&M college, standing in ROTC officer's uniform, riding boots, jodhpurs, and a Sam Browne belt over his tunic.

What made Carl smile was that the Lieutenant was wearing a sword and standing in front of a Texas flag. He looked like a general.

Carl slowly walked over to the table, the Lieutenant reading the pile of memos on his desk, and said weakly, "I'm having a problem at the Dispensary, Sir. I need some advice."

Looking up, the Lieutenant said, "Your hand is causing a problem?"

"Naw, Sir, it's my chest. I got a sharp pain," Carl said, feeling the top of his ears burn with embarrassment from exposing his problem. "I've been getting the <u>Macht</u> <u>Nichts</u> treatment from the German doctor at the Bamberg Dispensary.

"He's even threatened me with reporting me as malingering."

"How can I help?" the Lieutenant said, leaning back.

"I don't know," Carl said, "but I've been feeling lousy, Sir, for several months now -- and I'm losing weight. It feels like I have a deep cold -- and it won't go away."

The Lieutenant nodded, waiting for Carl to go on.

"I talked them into giving me an x-ray at the Nuremberg Hospital, but they told me they'd send it to the Bamberg Dispensary. I have to face that German doctor again," Carl said, looking at the ceiling of the hut, "and he's giving me the run-around."

"The Regiment will be back in Bamberg by next week," the Lieutenant said calmly, "why don't you wait until then -- see what the x-ray shows. Can you wait until we get back to Bamberg and get the x-ray report?"

"I guess so, Sir," Carl said, feeling the excitement cooling, by talking about the disease bothering him.

"What is it," the Lieutenant said, leaning forward over the table on his elbows, you think you have?"

"Emphysema maybe, Sir, or possibly -- TB."

"You don't look like -- a consumptive," the Lieutenant said.

"I know, Sir, but whatever it is -- I can't shake it off. I feel so lousy -- it must be something like TB. Long time now -- I feel tired all the time."

"The x-ray should show if you have it or not," the Lieutenant said, in a tone that indicated he would say no more. "Don't you think, Private Breckles?"

"Yes, Sir."

"How's that hand coming along?"

"It's much better, Sir. But I really can't tell. I've got so used to wearing the cast -- I can't tell."

Suddenly, Carl was beginning to see the Army's perspective of him: a hand in a cast, and now he's complaining about chest pains. He was overloading the Army's capacity to believe his complaints. He could see why the Army could judge him as someone shirking duty with medical complaints.

"Come back with the x-ray results," the Lieutenant said. "I want to know." He picked up a folder, opening it.

"Yes, Sir."

"And," the lieutenant said, "the Officer of the Day will be showing up -- any minute. You can go to your barracks tonight -- I'll be here to answer phone calls."

"Yes, Sir."

The Long Tom cannon fired again, as Carl was putting on his field jacket to go outside. After the shockwave passed, he walked to the hut door, feeling he did not get any help from the Lieutenant.

*   *   *   *   *

Two days after the Regiment moved back to Bamberg from the training grounds in Grafenwhore, Carl was at his desk in the Headquarters building, when Johnson, the clerk from Fox Company, walked in carrying a letter.

"Lasslett sent this letter to our Company," he said, holding the envelope out to Carl over his desk. "He asked me to pass it along to you."

"Hey, thanks for bringing it over," Carl said, taking the envelope.

"You know," Johnson said, pushing up his steel army eyeglasses on his nose, "I think he sort of asked for it -- the six-months in the slammer."

Johnson talked out the side of his mouth, and it gave drama to his speaking.

"How you figure that?"

"You know," Johnson said, stepping back from Carl's desk. "Ever since Fort Riley -- he's been doing things -- the Army told him not to do

"Yeah, I see what you mean."

"You two are buddies," Johnson said, "so I won't say anymore. If you need help with the typing load -- keep me in mind up here at Regiment, okay?"

"Yeah, yeah," Carl said watching him go to the door.

No more than Johnson went out, Flannery came through the door, carrying two sugar donuts on a napkin.

"Want one?" Flannery asked, holding them out.

"No thanks," Carl said getting up from his desk. He went over to the coffee pot on a side table and filled his cup.

"The PX Cafeteria is packed already," Flannery said sitting down at his desk, looking at the donuts, "they got liver and onions for dinner today at the Mess Hall."

"I don't blame them," Carl said picking up the envelope, then sitting down, "nobody likes liver and onions,"

"What'd Johnson want?" Flannery said, breaking a donut. "Was he asking about helping us do the typing?"

"Yeah." Carl opened the letter. "And he brought this letter from Lasslett."

The letter was written on a page out of a notebook.

> I hear you been seeing my wife.
> When I get out of this Stockade
> I'm going to shoot your ass for
> sleeping with her.

Carl sat for a moment, looking at the note.

"Hey," Flannery said, biting the donut, "you look pale. Is it bad news in the letter?"

"Yeah," Carl said sliding the note back in the envelope. "Lasslett wants me -- to loan some money. I can't help -- I can't even make it from payday to payday."

"Yeah," Flannery said picking up the second donut, "the seventy bucks we get from the army every month don't go very far."

The old Major came out of the Colonel's office.

"I need three copies of both these repots," he said walking to Carl's desk. "Type them and bring them to my office as soon as they're done," he said, handing two sheets to Carl. Then going to Flannery, he handed him two sheets.

"I want them in Distribution before noon."

"Yes, Sir," Carl said, as the major walked to his office.

As he was rolling three sheets of paper with carbons in between into the typewriter, Carl thought a moment; he would send word to Lasslett he was wrong about his wife and him.

He wondered who had told Lasslett that his wife was seen talking with him. Maybe someone in the PX Cafeteria, or maybe one of the women dependents on the bus to Nuremberg.

He would never know, that was for sure, he thought, and began typing.

"Word travels fast," he said quietly, "especially -- when it's gossip -- of the dirty kind."

*   *   *   *   *

Later that day, Carl heard the German doctor was back in the Dispensary from his weeklong medical conference in Frankfort, and was seeing patients.

"It's show-down time with this kraut doctor," Carl said, feeling his face flush, as he walked on the cobblestone roadway to the Dispensary. "This doctor must have been in medical school when Hitler was in power -- I wonder if that's got anything to do with it? -- maybe -- maybe he's some kind of nut for obeying orders."

Jackie, carrying the baby, came out the door as Carl started up the steps.

"How's the baby doing?" he said, trying not to show being surprised.

"She's got a swelling around the right eye now," Jackie said, holding the baby's face toward him. "On the same side as that ear. The doctors think it's some kind of viral infection -- working its way through her system -- they're giving her penicillin. I just came for a refill."

"Wow," Carl said, "she's sure having a rough time. Maybe she was bit by some bug -- or something."

"They're not sure," Jackie said moving the blanket to cover the child's face, "so I keep bringing her for the doctors to check -- every couple of days."

"Have you heard from Mike?" Carl asked.

"Yeah, the other day, I got a letter," Jackie said, quickly.

She was standing near the door of the Dispensary, and had to move aside, as a woman in a wheelchair was being pushed out of the waiting room.

Carl thought of the letter he got, the threat, but he said nothing.

"He's got to simmer down," Jackie said, shifting the baby, "his letter was sort of -- wild. He's got too much time to think, there in prison. He's -- sort of -- imagining things."

For a moment, Jackie stopped talking, watching the woman being lifted out of the wheelchair, being carried by two orderlies to a waiting car.

"Mike must be causing trouble in that prison," she said, looking at Carl again. "He wrote, they made him bow down -- put his nose on a line on the floor -- for two hours -- some kind of punishment.

"You're his friend, Carl," Jackie said shifting the weight of the child to her hip, "you could say things that would calm him down -- give him advice -- he listens to you."

"There's not much I can say," Carl said, slow, trying to find a way of not getting involved. He could not tell her about the threat in the letter he got.

"Mike says he wants to come home," Jackie said looking down at the baby, "he thinks -- he can help make her ear better. That's crazy. How can he come home?"

"You can't blame him for that," Carl said. "He just wants to help."

Jackie leaned her shoulder toward Carl, and said quietly, "I should not tell, but he says he's going to escape -- break out of jail -- and come home."

Carl made a face like he was about to whistle.

"Ah-h," he said. "Mike's not serious."

"I wrote him not to do anything foolish -- make more trouble," Jackie said rocking the child back and forth. "I didn't even tell him about her eye."

"All I can do, Jackie, is write him to soldier - on -- and let time pass."

Carl had been deliberately not looking at her face, all the time they had been talking, but now, he felt himself getting more involved with her. He was not sure -- if that was the place he wanted to be.

"Mike will listen to you," Jackie said, as she started down the Dispensary steps. "I'm counting on you to write him, Carl."

"I will," Carl said, thinking he would deny sleeping with her in his note. "I will," he said, turning to go in the door of the Dispensary.

In the Examining Room, the German doctor took the x-rays out of a large envelope, and put one on a lighted panel on a table, flat, like a map.

"You see," he said to Carl with a hint of satisfaction, "there are no lesions -- dark spots -- anywhere on the lungs."

Carl, taller than the doctor, looked first at the top of his head, the long black hair combed straight back, then bent lower, studying one side of the chest x-ray.

He saw shadows on the film, globules, but faint.

"What are these -- shadows?" Carl asked running his finger over the spots. "They cover part of the lung here, and over here."

"That must be spots made by the fluid for developing the film," the doctor said looking. "If you had lesions that size -- you would be very sick -- an advanced disease.

"No," he said looking at Carl, "I think the developing fluid used -- dried -- making these deposits that look like lesions."

"You said that before when I was here," Carl said, "and I feel more fatigued now, than before."

When he asked the doctor to view the lateral x-rays, the doctor slid the side-view of the lungs on the light-panel, and Carl looked closely.

"There are the spots again," Carl said straightening up from looking at the light panel. "In the same place. Dry developing fluid, bullshit," Carl said. "I should have more x-rays, and have them examined by someone who knows what to look for."

"You create a disturbance at this clinic," the doctor said, "every time you come here. I must remind you, that I can report you -- as a malingerer -- if you continue speaking like this."

Carl thought a moment, then said, "Couldn't you just say -- I'm requesting a second opinion?"

"That is not the procedure," the doctor said snapping off the light panel briskly. "You have been examined -- twice -- and found not to be sick, private -- fit for duty."

"I'm not convinced," Carl said, "that there is nothing wrong inside my chest -- I just don't feel well."

The doctor walked over to his desk and sat down, "we must wait -- to see if you improve -- or no."

Carl watched him writing on the papers in his file folder.

"Two week," the doctor said, not looking up from his writing. "You can report for an examination."

"If I'm still alive then," Carl said, pulling down his Eisenhower jacket, that slid up when he was looking at the x-rays.

CHAPTER 12

Carl sat looking out the train window on the way to Munich, thinking about the letter he sent Lasslett. He told about his fight with the doctor, and explained he had only seen Jackie at the PX, shopping. He hoped the letter would calm him down.

Lieutenant Taylor gave three-day passes to both Carl and Flannery for the office night work they did at Grafenwhore. They were talking about both of them going to Paris at the Enlisted Men's Club. But Carl decided not to go -- lack of money -- and Flannery went alone, taking a bus tour. Later, Carl and Margerite were talking, and she invited him to come visit Schwabing, where she lived in Munich. Schwabing is a district of Munich similar to Greenwich Village.

"You can stay at the room above my apartment in Munich," Margerite said at the Club that night. "I rent it for storage -- my jewelry supply. There are boxes -- everywhere -- but there is a bed you can use."

Carl had to smile, thinking of the last letter from his father, when he asked for money:

"Tell the Army I can't afford the cost to keep you in Europe. Tell them to send you home," he remembered his father writing.

Bending forward on the train seat, Carl unzipped his AWOL bag on the floor, and took out the liter bottle of cognac he bought at the station. He took a long drink.

It was not good cognac, and it burned going down, but it made his chest feel warm. It was the only remedy that worked. Being tired was another problem. He rested as much as he could back in Bamberg, lying down on his cot during the day.

Looking out the train window again, Carl enjoyed the warmth of the cognac, while looking ahead up the tracks where the flat country changed to rise in hills, and in the distance were purple mountains. Everything outside was brown, and there were patches of snow.

He grew drowsy, and while thinking he had to get another x-ray, fell asleep.

It was near noon in the noisy Munich Bonhoff, when Carl stepped down from the train car.

Margerite walked up wearing a raincoat and large floppy hat, looking like a pre-war movie star.

Carl had not seen her for two days; she left Bamberg on business -- a jewelry shipment coming from Dubrovnik, she said.

"You look handsome in civilian clothes," she said smiling.

"I'm only a 'civilian' for three days," he said, fluttering his raincoat over the tweed jacket, feeling a bit self-conscious.

"Do you have a suitcase?"

"No. Just my AWOL bag," he said holding it up. "I brought a clean shirt and socks -- and some shaving stuff."

"Come," she said, as if she did not hear what he had in the bag, taking hold of his arm, "we can get a taxi to my apartment -- then we get a lunch."

Walking next to her, Carl could feel the rhythm of her steps, interrupted but a slight pause in her movement, that she told him once was a hip injury caused by a fall from a horse.

He never thought to ask her about it.

She was still attractive, Carl thought, but the youthful glow was gone. She was in her early thirties, he guessed.

He had to ask himself why she chose him. There was a whole camp in Bamberg of soldiers asking her for a date at the Club. Then there was Sergeant Bowman, her boss, who could use his position to pressure her for favors.

Riding in the taxi, Carl was about to ask her why she asked him to Munich, when she suddenly said, "I will introduce you to my daughter, Katrina, when we get to the apartment."

She spoke softly, adding, "She is four years old."

"Hey," Carl said, turning to look at the side of her face where her pale-blond hair showed from under her big hat, "I didn't know you had a daughter."

"Yes, the wife of my business partner looks after her during the day. My partner, his wife, and their daughter, live in the apartment next to mine."

Carl remembered, she said her husband was killed in the bombing of Dresden. He was a veterinarian. That was ten years ago, Carl thought. Who was the father of the old daughter?

Turning away from her, looking out the taxi window, he told himself to forget all this background stuff about her, and enjoy himself here in Munich.

They were passing a three-story beer hall with a large sign in gold lettering: <u>LOWENBRAU</u>.

"What is this <u>Schwabing</u> place all about?" he asked, rubbing the spot on his chest where the dull ache came again.

"It is bohemian," she said smiling, looking at him, "a place for artists -- painters and poets -- and some students from the university. They all live here -- making an artist colony, like the Greenwich Village in New York."

"Artists are wild," Carl said, "and they like to have fun. Are they like that here?"

"The Badenwenner is a dance club," Margerite said, taking hold of his hand, looking at him. "We can go there this evening. You will see."

When the taxi stopped in front of an old stone building, a wide arch over the front door, Carl, looking up, said "This place looks like a museum."

"Here we are, Carl, thirteen Georgstrasse. Remember the address."

"Okay," Carl said, leaning to get his wallet out of his back pocket. "How much we owe for the taxi?"

"No, no," Margerite said, holding his arm, "I pay -- I get the business deduction -- the driver knows."

Carl did not understand, but he felt a relief. He had only brought twenty-six Marks for expenses.

Going up the steps to the stone building door, Carl said, "Letting me use your spare room, is a big savings -- I wouldn't have been able to come --"

"I know soldier's are not paid much, Carl, you do not have to say anything about money. Just enjoy Munich."

Pulling open the door into the lobby, she said, "The room is on the third floor. You can put your bag there, and after lunch, I make a quick delivery -- and I show you Munich when we go."

Margerite opened the door of an apartment on the second floor, and Carl saw a heavy woman, standing with a little girl with blond hair that was almost white.

The girl ran to her mother. Margerite, smiling, saying something in German, turned the child around by the shoulders to face Carl.

"This is Katrina," Margerite said to Carl, smiling.

"Hello," he said bending down, holding out his hand. "Guten Tag, Katrina."

"Tag," the child said softly, and after shaking hands, quickly leaned back against her mother.

"She is tired," the heavy woman said in English. "It is her time for a nap."

"This is Frau Kirschner," Margerite said to Carl, who nodded to the heavy woman, leading the child out of the room.

"And there at the table," Margerite said pointing to the dining room, "is Victor -- my business partner -- who is also a professional accountant."

"Hello," Carl said to the nearly bald man in an open white shirt sitting at the dining table. There were papers scattered on the table, and a large open ledger book.

"Welcome to Munich," Victor said, getting up halfway out of his chair, almost making a bow.

Carl sensed the man was nervous; he was upset about something. His movements were too abrupt.

"Come," Margerite said, taking hold of Carl's arm holding the AWOL bag, "I show you where you can sleep."

He followed her up a flight of dark steps, and when she swung open the door, snapping on the light, he said, "Hey, this is great."

He stood looking at the large bed, and the two rows of cardboard boxes, stacked neatly almost to the ceiling, along the wall. To the left was a bathroom with a tub.

"No one will bother you," Margerite said. "They stay downstairs. They don't come up -- only me," she said, smiling.

"I'm glad to hear that," Carl said, dropping his AWOL bag on the bed.

He put his arms around Margerite and kissed her slowly.

"We must act -- sensible," she said, before he kissed her again. "They will be watching us," she said to his face. "You understand --" she said as he kissed her neck, "don't you?"

"Yes," Carl said, pulling open her raincoat.

"No, no," she said backing up, "not now, please." She closed her coat, holding her arms in front. "Not now -- I have business this afternoon -- and we must have a lunch," she said holding him at arm's length. "You understand? -- you must understand."

"Okay, okay, I get the message," Carl said.

"Come," Margerite said, straightening her coat, "we deliver some jewelry -- to the club in the paratrooper camp outside Munich. You can see the city as we drive."

"I could use a drink," Carl said, rubbing his chest.

"After," Margerite said stepping to the door. "My delivery is very important. The paratroopers are having a party tonight -- and my assistant must have a good supply of jewelry for her tables at the club."

"Business comes first," Carl said. "It's important -- all over the world."

"We only take an hour, Carl. Then we are done."

"Okay," he said, thinking of the bottle of cognac in his AWOL bag. "Let me wash my face -- comb my hair," he said. "I'll be down in a minute."

"Yes. I go down and load the van," Margerite said going to the door. "We use my partner's Volkswagen microbus."

When she was gone out of the room, Carl took a quick drink of cognac, then feeling it go down warmly, took a long drink, wishing it would hold him for the afternoon.

Margerite was pointing out the landmarks in Munich, when Carl suddenly quipped, "So this is where the Third Reich began, huh?"

After he said it, he realized he was almost accusing Margerite of having something to do with it.

"Yes," she said, "the beer stube is still here -- the building, where they had their first meetings -- but now -- the name is changed. I show you."

She turned the boxy van off the busy street onto a gloomy side street.

"There is the place -- just there. It is a Keller -- a downstairs place -- that is where National Socialism began."

Carl sat up, looking, "So that's where Hitler and his gang held their first meetings."

"Yes, he began the political movement that became the Nazi Party there -- the fights with other political parties were called putsches."

"None of our bombs hit this neighborhood," Carl said.

"No," Margerite said while turning at the next corner.

It was an overcast day, making the stone buildings of Munich seem dreary to Carl. The cold damp seemed to make his chest ache worse. He sat quietly, wishing he had his cognac bottle, looking at the city giving way to the suburbs and open space.

"There is the paratrooper caserne," Margerite said pointing off to the right of the road. "This will not take long."

On his left Carl saw a metal bar gate with crooked letters in an arch: ARBIET MACHT FREI.

"Hey, is that a concentration camp?" he asked, sitting up.

"Yes, Dachau."

"Damn," Carl said quietly, staring at the gate. "A death camp right in the suburbs. And people said -- they didn't know what was going on here."

Margerite was silent as she turned the bus off the road, onto a street that ran uphill on a grassy slope, where up ahead loomed a three-story army barracks.

She stopped at the guardhouse and began digging in her purse for her gate pass.

"Pass, please," a guard in a white helmet asked her through the open bus window.

She held up a plastic card, saying "I am delivering to the Enlisted Men's Club."

Carl thought he would be asked to show his Army AGO card, but the guard said, "The Club is up the road and to the right," and waved them through.

Carl said, as they drove toward the buildings, "How can these guys sleep at night -- with that Dachau place across the road over there?"

"Things are different now," Margerite said. "For sure."

Both the cardboard boxed were light, but awkward for Carl, as he followed Margerite up the steps of the club to a storeroom.

Back outside, Margerite was sliding the side door of the van closed, when she said, "Now we get something to eat."

"I need a beer," Carl said just as she was starting the van, "I mean -- after all that work."

"I know a place you will like," she said, smiling, shifting the van into gear.

Passing Dachau again, Carl was closer this time on his side of the road to the death camp, but he turned away not wanting to look, rubbing his chest in the center.

He looked at Margerite driving, thinking she was a teenager, when the Third Reich was running Germany. You cannot blame her. What could <u>anyone</u> do that lived here? He shook his head, as if to get rid of the thought that with the concentration camp so close to Munich, everybody must have known what was going on.

Looking at Margerite's stringy blond hair and her classic face, he wished suddenly he could have met her when she was younger.

A wave of fatigue was pressing down on Carl now, as they were coming back into Munich, and he turned his face to the window and closed his eyes.

"If Victor did not need the van," Margerite said as they were driving in the city, "I would show you all the sites of Munich."

"Oh," Carl said opening his eyes, "If he needs the van -- that's okay. We can spend more time -- downtown."

"Yes, but we must eat something," she said insisting. "I stop for only a few minutes. You will see."

"I could use a drink instead," Carl said looking at the stone buildings they were passing.

"You drink maybe too much, Carl. Do you agree?"

Carl made a long face at her.

With the giant train station ahead, Margerite turned the van to the inside road lane, along the curb, then stopped next to a lunch wagon with lettering: <u>WURST</u>.

"There is lunch," she said pointing.

"Here? We passed this Bahnhof when I came to town. This hot-dog stand too."

"The wurst is delicious -- homemade -- you will thank me, Carl," she said opening the van door to get out.

Margerite spoke to the fat vendor in an apron over his jacket, and he gave her a white sausage in a bun, and a Vienna sausage in another.

Back in the van they were both eating.

"They are good, you're right," Carl said before he took another bite. He liked the mustard, not yellow, but brown and spicy. "I should have got two."

Margerite bit the end off her white wurst, and while chewing, started the van engine.

She held the sausage and bun, wrapped in a napkin, aloft in her hand, gracefully, while concentrating on driving. Carl, watching her, thought she looked elegant, very feminine, and she made him smile.

"We are a little bit late," she said. "Victor will be upset -- he has an appointment -- with a client."

Carl grinned, looking at her. He wanted to put out his hands and take hold of her.

Victor was standing, waiting in the parking lot behind Margerite's apartment building.

"There's your business partner," Carl said wiping his fingers with the napkin. "He looks worried."

"We are twenty minutes late," Margerite said flatly, while driving up to Victor, dressed in a dark green Loden coat, holding a flat briefcase.

Margerite spoke rapidly in German to Victor, as she climbed out of the van, and when he spoke back, Carl heard the word "Ursula," in their conversation as he stood near the van.

Then Margerite showed frustration by dropping both arms suddenly, as if defeated, as she watched Victor climb into the van.

"What's the matter?" Carl asked her, as she looked at the sausage and napkin she held.

"The mother of the girl Ursula that works for me at the paratrooper camp -- had a heart attack. Ursula is going to the hospital -- and I must work tonight in her place," Margerite said, throwing away what was left of her sausage into a trash barrel.

"I am sorry," Margerite said, walking with Carl to the back entrance of the apartment building, "but I cannot show you the nightlife in Munich -- tonight."

"Macht Nichts," Carl said, glancing up at the wet building in front of him, suddenly thinking of the bed upstairs. "I feel tired now, like an elephant is sitting on me. Later, if I feel better, I might go out and walk around town," he said pulling open the door for Margerite.

Going up the stairs inside, Margerite stopped, and holding Carl's arm, "I don't have to go to the camp until four," she said. "We can go to town -- now -- if you like. Take a taxi."

Looking at his watch, Carl saw it was almost one-thirty and shrugged.

"Yeah, okay," Carl said fighting fatigue that seemed to be coming in waves.

"We can go to the Hofbrau Haus," Margerite said, and kissed him. "I know you -- will like -- that place."

He put his arms around her and kissed her until she pushed him away, smiling.

Sitting at the heavy wood table in the beer hall, Carl could not help watching two fat women at the next table, as they were eating something, cutting off pieces of something spiral-cut, like an accordion.

"What the hell are they eating?" Carl asked, leaning over his tall glass beer stein, whispering to Margerite.

"Oh," Margerite said, "that's radish -- a very large one. You break off from the spiral -- dip in the rock salt, and eat it. It make you -- more thirsty for beer."

"Very practical," Carl said.

After his second liter of beer in the tall glass stein, he began to get drowsy.

Then Margerite said, "I must go -- dress for work at my apartment." She was looking at her watch. "You can stay."

"Okay," Carl said slowly nodding, feeling the effect of the beer, "maybe I'll stay -- and have another mug of beer. It makes me feel better."

"It is unfortunate I must go," Margerite said, pulling on her raincoat as she stood next to the table, "but Ursula cannot be blamed.

"We have tomorrow -- all day -- to see the city."

"Come up to my room," Carl said, "when you come back from work," looking up at her. "No matter how late -- wake me."

He took her hand for a moment.

She nodded.

When she turned to walk away, he did not get up, he was too tired. He sat alone, feeling an odd sense of relief, watching her go. He was alone with his tiredness now. He did not make excuses, or explain it to anyone.

Later, walking outside the beer hall, he saw a theater across the street showing "THREE PENNY OPERA." A sign boasted a German film with English sub-titles. A Kurt Weil Musical.

"I heard a lot about that flick," he said. "Why not go see it? Kill some time."

He bought a ticket, and after a few minutes, sitting in the dark, listening to the quickstep music, he fell asleep.

CHAPTER 13

Getting out of the taxi he had taken from the "Three Penny Opera" movie, Carl paid the driver and pulled his raincoat collar tight, up to his neck. The night air was cold, adding to his guilt.

He had been trying to discover how he caught this Tuberculosis disease. He kept thinking about it -- now and again -- hoping he would stumble on the source of his lung trouble. He would think back sometimes of where he was, and who he was with in the past, looking for an answer.

He could not explain why, but being here in Munich made him angry about having the disease.

"How could the doctors at the Enlistment Center back in Detroit overlook such a serious disease like Tuberculosis?" he asked himself, going up the steps of Margerite's apartment building. "Or, maybe I didn't have it then. Maybe I got it while in the Army."

"Now, things are worse," he said ringing the bell to have the buzzer unlock the door to the apartment house lobby. "Now I got to convince the army -- I have the damn disease."

He remembered reading a pamphlet about Tuberculosis in the Nuremberg Army hospital. It said the disease took nearly a year to "incubate" in your lungs.

The buzzer rang, and he opened the door and walked into the lobby.

"I've been in the army -- almost two years," he said muttering to himself, crossing the lobby to the stairs. "How do you explain that?" he said out loud.

Going slow up the steps, he muttered, "the only conclusion is -- I got that damn bug from someone -- in the army. But who, dammit? Or maybe it was a German?"

In the bedroom he hung his raincoat on the top edge of the bathroom door, and draping his tweed sports jacket over the back of a chair, he said out loud "Maybe I could go to a German civilian doctor -- a lung specialist? Naw, that would cost -- I don't have that kind of money. A specialist is expensive. Besides -- the Army would probably have a fit."

Sitting down on the bed, he unzipped the AWOL bag and took a long drink quickly from the cognac bottle.

He choked, feeling the cheap cognac burn all the way to his stomach. "Blah," he said, undressed, dropped on the bed, lying on his side.

He fell asleep after struggling to pull the featherbed quilt over himself, half lying on it, too tired to get up and pull it over his entire body.

Later, he woke up feeling wetness against the side of his face on the pillow.

Reaching over, he turned on the table lamp to look.

"Puke -- ugh," he said, quickly wiping the side of his face with his hand. "I must have vomited -- in my sleep."

Moving into the bathroom, he washed his face with cold water, and looking in the mirror, said, "Damn, it's even in my hair -- what a mess."

After washing his hair clean in the basin again, he walked back to the bed, seeing the pillow and the reddish mess where his head had been.

Feeling embarrassed for what he had done, he slipped off the pillowcase, and washing it in the sink, saw there were lumps, particles of undigested food in the fluid.

"What a way to wake up," he said while dropping the pillowcase over the wood frame of the bed stand to dry. "I'm lucky I woke up -- I could have drowned -- or something. Yeah, I could have drowned in my own puke.

"I'm sick as hell. I could even die," he said to himself, sitting down on the bed. Then he lay back down, pulling the clean pillow under his head. "Man, I feel tired," he said looking at his watch, "and it's only eleven-twenty."

He fell asleep again, leaving the light on.

He woke suddenly, when he heard the bedroom door open, and looked up to see Margerite. She was carrying a champagne bottle by the neck.

"Shush," she said quietly closing the door, "don't wake them up -- downstairs." Holding up the champagne bottle, she said smiling, "They had a wedding at the paratrooper club -- I took this."

Coming over to the bed, she saw the wet pillowcase.

"Pillowcase?" she asked pointing with the bottle. "You were sick?"

"A little," Carl said leaning up on one arm. "I rinsed it out."

"Is that why you have the light on?"

"Sort of."

He could see she was drunk, when she tried to pull the champagne bottle through the sleeve of her coat, as she took it off. She flung the coat over the bedstead next to the pillowcase.

"You must have joined the wedding celebration," he said, glancing at his watch. "It's almost one o'clock."

"I always get tipsy at weddings," she said setting the bottle on the nightstand. "I always drink -- too much at weddings."

She sat down on the bed next to him, while taking off her hat, then dropping it on the floor.

"An unmarried woman -- goes to a wedding," she said taking hold of the bottle. "and she pretends -- she is the next to be married."

"That's too complicated for me," Carl said. "There's a corkscrew on my utility knife -- it's in my AWOL bag -- here by the bed."

When he leaned over the side of the bed, Margerite kissed the back of his neck.

He sat up holding the knife, and with the other hand in the short wrist cast, reached, pulling her close, kissing her hard, feeling her face burning.

He dropped the knife, making a <u>thud</u> sound.

"Shush," she whispered. "Do not wake them downstairs," her voice interrupted with heavy breathing.

Carl slipped his hand under her sweater between her breasts, and was pulling at her bra.

She turned and snapped off the light. There was an almost silent <u>swish</u> of nylon on nylon, and suddenly she was undressed and laying next to him on the bed.

Her skin was burning where it touched Carl, pulling off his clothes, and he did not feel tired as she clung against him, writhing; he was invigorated by her heat.

An odor rose from her, as she climbed astride Carl and he felt wetness between her legs. She was groping between Carl's legs, and then he felt her put him inside her.

He began thrusting, moving with her doing the same, in abrupt, almost frenzy motions.

"Lieb -- ling. Liebling," she moaned in her throat as if not talking to him.

He took hold of her breasts, when she leaned back, her mouth open, head back, pushing herself against him in jerking motions, almost in a contorted position above him.

When Carl released in her, his climax, she gave out a silent moan as if in pain.

They were both wet with perspiration, and as she moved to lay next to him, he could feel her taunt body, like a graceful animal, tight, sinuous, all spent. She had given her all.

Carl, still breathing heavy, put his good hand to her face, pushing back the wet hair on the side of her face.

"Hope," he whispered, "they didn't hear us, downstairs," when she turned her face to his.

"I could not -- contain -- myself," she whispered back. "At the wedding -- everything was a passion. The married couple -- you could see the wanting of the bride and groom. Everyone -- became excited -- watching their -- desire."

"Yeah," Carl whispered, "but I think we made a noise -- I mean the bed, made a lot of noise. Your business partner and his wife -- must have heard us --"

She leaned up on one elbow, her breasts touching his face, the nipples hard, whispering, "That Victor has been after me for years -- he is too nervous -- a woman does not want sex with a nervous man."

Running his thumb on her nipple, holding the breast in his good hand, Carl whispered, "and what about Sergeant Bowman? Woman are usually attracted to their boss."

"You have seen the Sergeant's stomach. That is not sexy."

"What about the other soldiers in the Club at Bamberg?" Carl asked, whispering, feeling Margerite moving to make herself comfortable laying on her side.

He was fishing for the reason she had singled him out, from all the others at the Club in Bamberg.

"Their faces," she whispered. "Most of them -- have stupid faces."

"Ah-h," Carl said to her ear, "and I don't have a stupid face."

"No," she whispered, putting a hand on his mouth. "You have an -- intelligent face."

She kissed Carl, lying against him, reaching to turn on the light.

"That was some wedding you went to tonight," Carl whispered, saying it like a wisecrack. "The paratrooper Club must have been wild."

"It was as if the paratrooper and the bride," Margerite said in a distant tone, as if not speaking to Carl, "were born for one another. When they were married, it was just a -- formality.

"They seemed -- already married -- back in time. Everyone could see this, how they -- longed -- for each other. This excited everyone."

"Okay," Carl said grinning. "I believe you."

Smoothing her hair back from her face with her hands, Margerite said distantly, "I would like a glass of champagne."

While Carl was uncorking the champagne, Margerite went into the bathroom and washed and came back with a towel around her waist.

Carl watched her coming back to the bed, liking the way she moved her lanky body; thin arms, thin legs, not round and curvy like other women. She was like an athlete, who moved with purpose, despite the hitch in her step from the hip injury.

"We don't have any glasses," he said, popping open the champagne.

"There, in that China cabinet," Margerite said pointing, as she sat down on the edge of the bed. "Victor's wife stores her glassware."

Carl opened the wood door of the cabinet, and saw a display of China bowls, dishes, and glasses of every size.

"These will do the job," he said selecting two tulip-shaped glasses.

"They are perfect, Carl. We celebrate our -- wedding."

Carl shrugged, not speaking, and grinning poured the champagne slowly into the glasses, as if he did not hear her "wedding" remark.

"Thank you for tonight," she said, sipping the champagne, watching Carl drink his down, and refilling the glass.

"What are you thanking me for?" Carl asked, before downing the second glass.

"I -- have not made love -- for -- a long time," she said in a low voice, holding her glass in front of her face.

"How long a time?" Carl asked grinning.

"I don't answer that question," she said and sipped her drink. "And -- you should not ask."

The champagne helped Carl not feel his fatigue, but for some reason, it was and effort for him to move.

Finishing the champagne in his glass, he set it on the floor, then lay back on the bed, crossways, his head touching the wall.

"I feel like a ton of bricks is sitting on me," he said, reaching to put his hand on Margerite's bare back. "Damn, I'm tired. Wiped out."

"But you are here in Munich," Margerite said quietly, as she stood up, and bending gracefully, picked up Carl's empty glass on the floor, "and I want you to see the city -- you have the opportunity. You must make an effort."

He watched her set the two glasses on the dresser near the bathroom doorway, then pull on her blouse, leaving it open.

"Don't get dressed," Carl said, holding out his good hand to her. "Come back to bed."

"This room is cold, Carl," she whispered.

"Come back to bed," he said lifting the down bedcover, while swinging his legs off the end of the bed, and drawing them up.

His hand in the cast hit the wall with a <u>clump</u> sound.

"Careful with that hand," she said sliding under the quilt, the full length of her against him again, "you are going to wake them up downstairs. My daughter gets up -- early."

"Sometimes," Carl said, "I forget I still have the cast on."

"Yes," Margerite said resting her chin on Carl's chest, "you have been changing -- lately. You are becoming more -- forgetful of things. You seem -- isolated -- from people."

"I'm just tired," Carl said, while thinking that was not a strong enough excuse not to tour Munich, "right down to my socks."

"I must go downstairs," she said, moving up her body to face Carl. "I should be downstairs when they wake up."

He moved his hands down her back to her bottom, and held it hard against himself.

"Let's make love again," he whispered.

"No, not now, Carl. You must understand."

"I understand we can't be together when we want," he said.

"We should be married -- and go to the 'States, Carl. Then we could do what we want -- all the time."

She rose up on her arms, looking at him, as if struck by an idea. "If me and my daughter were in the 'States, we could open a store -- sell jewelry -- and you would not have to work."

There is was in a nutshell, Carl thought. It came out. What Margerite wants, why she selected me out of all the soldiers in Bamberg; I am her ticket to the United States.

"But what about now?" Carl asked. "Can't we make love now?"

"If you are gravely sick, as you claim, Carl, then maybe it is not good for you -- too much -- making love."

She sat up, putting her hand on his chest.

"Yes I could die right here in bed. Killed by love."

"Be serious, Carl," she said, getting out of bed, then getting dressed. "I have responsibilities -- to others. Please, don't embarrass me downstairs."

"I wouldn't think if it."

Standing at the door, opening it, Margerite said, "Come for coffee, downstairs. When you are ready."

When the door closed, Carl reached under the bed for the cognac bottle in his AWOL bag.

Holding it up to the light, he said, "Only about a third left," and removed the cork with the hand in a cast.

After a long drink, then a short one, he laid back, the bottle in his armpit.

"Man, I feel like I'm crushed," he said putting the cork back in the bottle. "Maybe if I sleep a little more -- I won't feel so bad."

He turned on his side, pulling the pillow over his head.

Margerite woke him, tapping on the bedroom door she held open, "I came to see if you are all right -- we heard a loud thump downstairs. Everyone is concerned for you."

The cognac bottle lay in the middle of the floor, and when Margerite bent to pick it up, Carl said, "Hey, give me that -- I need a swallow, bad."

When she handed him the bottle, he took a long drink, then checked, looked at what was left.

"You cannot lay in bed all day drinking, Carl. It is after ten o'clock, and everyone downstairs is nervous. They accuse me of bringing a drunken GI in the house."

Margerite was standing next to the bed, looking at him.

"I feel exhausted," Carl said looking up at her. "I dropped off to sleep, that's all. You can't blame me for being tired."

"You should get up now," Margerite said, folding her arms at her waist, pulling her clean tan blouse tight over her breasts. "You must behave like a house guest -- and not a drunken soldier on leave."

"Ah-h," Carl said taking her arm, pulling her down on the bed, "don't talk like that."

"Not now," Margerite said, twisting her arm out of his hand. "None of that."

"You've changed," Carl said, putting his bare feet down on the floor, "all of a sudden. How come?"

"That bump noise," she said backing up. "You frightened everyone downstairs -- they are afraid -- asking what you will do now. We must go out -- out of the house."

"Okay," Carl said, getting up from the bed. "I overstayed my welcome. I get it."

He pulled on his slacks, then his shirt, and was sitting on the edge of the bed, pulling on his socks, when Margerite said, "we can go for a walk in the city. It is early in the day -- a sunny Sunday morning."

"I'm too tired to be a tourist today," Carl said, tying his shoe. "I'm sick with something. I better get back to Bamberg and see an army doctor -- before I get worse. You can walk me to the train station."

"Are you sure about this?" Margerite asked looking down at him tying his other shoe.

He stood up and kissed her quickly on the lips.

"Thanks for everything," he said, lifting his sport jacket off the back of the chair. "You've given me a soldier's dream-three day pass, Margerite, but I've got to get back to Bamberg."

Pulling on the tweed jacket, he said softly, "Something bad is coming. I can _feel_ it."

"Don't talk like that, Carl. You make me afraid."

"Come with me to the Bohnhof," he said pulling on his raincoat. "I'm sorry you are afraid -- but, I'm afraid too."

CHAPTER 14

Carl had slept most of the way back to Bamberg on the train, but his cognac bottle was empty. He was looking for a wine shop, walking on the street away from the Bonhoff, carrying his AWOL bag in his good hand, feeling light headed.

It had stopped raining, and the sky was clearing now, people were looking in store windows, some sitting in the taverns near the train station, and he was glad to be back near camp.

He found a shop with wine and cognac bottles on a glass rack in the window. The shop was expensive, all the best brands, and he used most of his money to buy a liter of Ansback Urlaut cognac. Outside, he had put the bottle wrapped in a paper bag in his AWOL bag, zipping it up, and looking for a place to sneak a quick drink, when he heard, "Carl? Carl Breckles."

It was a woman's voice from across the street.

He turned, looking, and saw Jackie, Lasslett's wife, standing outside a market, holding four packs of cigarettes, in her hands.

"Hey," he said, crossing the street, walking up to her, "How you doing?"

At first he thought she was wearing too much make-up, then he saw it was dark circles under her eyes. She looked frail; her shoulders slumped.

"Have you heard?" she said, biting her lower lip, looking at him as if pleading.

"Heard what? I've just come back from Munich on a three-day pass. I just got here."

"Mike hanged himself," she said quietly, then looking away, as if to find some relief up the street, and began to cry.

"Wha-at? No. No," he said, standing with his mouth open in disbelief.

Jackie, nodding, looking at him now, "He hanged himself with a strip of blanket -- in his cell -- late at night," she said, her voice quivering. "Early Saturday. The Army phoned me."

"Ah-h," Carl said, dropping his eyes from starring at her, "that's unbelievable, Jackie."

"He was upset about the baby's ear infection," she said, her face contorted with trying to hold her crying back. "He wrote me a letter. He wanted to come home -- to help."

Carl stood for a moment, feeling like he had been punched in the stomach, unable to breath.

"The army wanted to send his body to the States, but I told them here was his home. Bury him here, so they are taking him to a military cemetery in France for burial."

Carl, unable to speak, took out his handkerchief, and shaking it open, handed it to her.

"I can't sleep," Jackie said wiping her face. "I smoke, lighting one cigarette after another. I ran out, so I came here to the store and bought four packs."

"Is there anything -- I can do to help, Jackie?"

Carl felt the question was trite, but he could think of nothing meaningful to say.

"Can you -- come talk for a while?" she said wiping one, then the other eye. "I got to talk -- or I'm going to go crazy."

"Okay. We'll go to a café."

"No, we don't have to go to a café. We can go to the apartment. It's just three blocks from here."

"All right," Carl said, nodding, quickly thinking the apartment would give him a chance to open the new bottle of cognac.

Jackie was crumpling Carl's handkerchief in her hand as they walked, making it into a ball, when she said, "You know Mike thought a lot of your opinions -- even back in Kansas at Fort Riley."

Carl nodded. "I should have talked to him over in Mannheim," he said slowly. "I might have saved him."

"I didn't get to visit him in prison either," Jackie said, pointing for them to turn at the corner as they walked. "I couldn't go with a sick child -- and I couldn't leave her home. But I feel I should have gone. My being there might have saved him. I don't know."

Carl shrugged, as if trying to rid himself of guilt, and looking at Jackie walking next to him, blurted, "Who knows for sure -- what you do -- or say -- how it affects people."

When they turned the corner, Carl saw they were walking in the old section of Bamberg. The buildings, like Shakespeare's time, were made with timbers and plaster, and some of them had wood balconies that hung out over the cobblestone street.

"Here's the apartment," Jackie said stopping, pointing with the hand holding the balled handkerchief.

Carl looked at the narrow door, where next to it was a shop window with a pair of tall tan boots on display in the window.

Jackie opened the door, and Carl, following, saw the door bottom was worn badly from scraping on the stone threshold.

Up in the apartment, as Carl walked through the door, he saw clothing stacked on the table and sofa, so he sat down in an overstuffed chair next to a window.

Jackie was unzipping her jacket, when she said, "I'm in the middle of packing all my things -- for the trip back to Wisconsin. My trunk and some suitcases are in the back bedroom. I'm almost done."

"Where's the baby?" Carl asked, opening the AWOL bag for the cognac.

"She's with Frau Kohler, the boot maker's wife, down the hall. They have a two-year old boy, and she takes care of Martha when I have to go out."

A church bell rang, a deep clanging, and Carl was startled; the sound came from close by.

"Wow," he said holding the cognac bottle, "this neighborhood is right out of the Medieval Ages. Like Notre Dame in Paris."

"Yeah," Jackie said, lighting a cigarette, "just down the street is Zur Dom -- a big church. They had a bishop, or cardinal here, who was some kind of knight-lord, and he went on one of the Crusades -- he left from here in Bamberg for the Holy Land."

"Okay," Carl said. "It's a real historic neighborhood you live in here."

"When you don't have much money," Jackie said quietly, "you have to live where you can afford. Especially if you don't have a government subsidy from the army."

Carl took his utility knife, and used the corkscrew to open the cognac bottle, when he said, "Can you get some glasses?"

Jackie pulled off her jacket quickly, her pointed breasts showing, when the jersey shirt she wore pulled tight.

Carl had caught the view of her, while lifting the cognac bottle for a quick sip. He watched her getting glasses from a cabinet.

"This is smooth," he said looking at the bottle. "It ought to be -- it costs enough."

"I don't drink much," Jackie said. "Just give me a little." She held out two glasses, "Maybe it will calm me down -- make me feel better."

He was seated in the chair, and after he gave her a little in her glass, he poured his half full, drinking, watching as she moved over to the window, and stood looking out.

"Aren't you going to get the baby?" he said, after adding a bit more cognac to his glass.

The Cognac made his tiredness drain away, but he knew it would only last as long as the cognac he had drunk.

"No. I don't want to wake her," she said looking across to the wall clock. "She still has half hour to go on her afternoon nap."

She was holding back her emotions. Carl could <u>feel</u> the pain welled up in her, by just watching.

"I miss Mike," she said and sipped her cognac. "All these weeks he's been in prison -- have been -- hell," she said quietly.

"Yeah," Carl said softly, "I can imagine."

"No you can't," she said, looking out the window.

"Right," he said.

"At night is the worst time," she said not looking at him. "I kept wondering how I was going to get through the next day -- and trying not to think there was six months ahead of me."

"That's rough," he said, putting the cork back in the cognac bottle, fumbling with his cast hand, then putting the bottle in his AWOL bag.

There was no way of helping her. He was trying to think of a way to leave. This was personal stuff she was spilling, and it made him uneasy. He was not prepared for it.

"I couldn't cheat on Mike," she said setting her glass down on a lamp table. She picked up a framed photograph, and held it for Carl to see.

Carl looked at the picture of Lasslett in a t-shirt, leaning on a pick-up truck fender, sleeves rolled, a James Dean haircut.

"I couldn't cheat on him," she said, "I mean -- while he was locked-up."

Carl felt the way you do watching a storm coming.

He stood up slowly from the overstuffed chair, and to distract her, said, "It'll be better for you -- when you get back home -- to Wisconsin. You and the baby have a place to go -- the change will help -- ease things."

He picked up his raincoat off the arm of the overstuffed chair.

"You're not leaving -- so soon, Carl?"

"I'm not feeling too good," he said while sliding on the raincoat, pushing the cast hand through the sleeve slowly. "That's why I came back from Munich -- early.

"I'm going to see a doctor tomorrow at the Dispensary. There's something wrong in my chest -- and I don't feel right."

"I hope nothing serious is wrong with you, Carl," Jackie said while moving to stand in front of the door. "But, why can't you stay a while longer?"

The strain on her face, in front of his, was almost unbearable for him to look at. She was pleading.

"Isn't it time for the baby to wake up?" he said, thinking fast. "I don't know what I've got in my chest. I wouldn't want to expose Martha to -- what I might have."

"But I've been alone for almost a month," she said looking down at the floor, pulling on her jersey shirt to make it tight. "And nobody -- but Frau Kohler for company. It's nice to have -- somebody I know -- to be with."

"Sorry I have to run," Carl said feeling the effect of the cognac draining away. "But, I'm not feeling good -- I've been this way for too long. I've got to do something about it."

"Okay, Carl," Jackie said. "I'm disappointed we didn't get to talk longer. You understand?"

She stepped aside, but watched him pull open the door.

"You'll feel better," Carl said, "when you get back to Wisconsin."

It was the only thing consoling he could think to say.

She began crying when he walked out the door, her following him out into the narrow hall.

"Take care of yourself," she said as he started down the stairs. "You were a good friend of Mike's."

He did not say anything, but felt a sense of relief, as he went down the narrow steps, going away.

*   *   *   *   *

Carl had been sleeping in his coat in the upstairs barracks of the Education Building for two hours, when Flannery came in and turned on the lights.

"Boy, I'm dog tired," he said, dropping his suitcase on the floor next to his footlocker. "I didn't get any sleep at <u>all</u> in Paris," he said sitting down heavy, on his cot. "We were on the town -- all night -- and I'm beat."

"I'm wiped-out too," Carl said, looking out of the bed covers. "Hey, you want a snort of cognac?"

"Not now," Flannery said, pulling off his sport coat while still sitting on his cot. "I've got to sack-out. I thought I could get some shut-eye on the bus coming back from Paris. But it stopped in Strasbourg on the French border, so everybody could take photos of some big cathedral."

Carl reached over, and sliding his AWOL bag out from under his cot, found the cognac bottle and took a drink.

"Did you get laid in Paris?" Carl asked, after swallowing the cognac, making a grimace face, feeling the burn.

"Naw," Flannery said, "they want you to buy a bottle of champagne -- and all that crap in those tourist traps. They think <u>all</u> Americans -- are rich."

Flannery took off one shoe, then the other, still sitting on his cot across the room, when he asked, "Did you make it with that Margerite from the Club -- down in Munich?"

"She's a tiger -- in the sack," Carl said while putting the cork back in the bottle with the hand in a cast.

"I don't like -- older women," Flannery said, standing up, and taking off his slacks, draping them on a hanger, the sport coat over them. "Hey, I got some news you'll be real interested in," he said while hanging the clothes in his upright closet.

"I got some news too," Carl said. "Lasslett hanged himself in prison. I met his wife, when I came out of the Bahnhof. She told me about it."

"No shit," Flannery said. "That poor bastard -- but it figures -- him being stuck there for six months.

"Hey, Carl, you didn't bang the wife too? She's a hot number," Flannery said pulling open the tightly made cot blankets so he could climb under. "A lot of guys -- have tried."

"Naw, but I could have," Carl said. "He was a buddy, so I passed it up -- they haven't even planted him yet, and she's off and running. It wouldn't be right."

"You should have," Flannery said, getting up again, to snap off the lights, and going back to bed, "because the way I hear it -- the Army wants to put you in Mannheim prison like they did Lasslett."

"What are you talking about?" raising his head in the dark.

"There was an MP Company Clerk on the tour bus, and when I told him I was from Fox Company, he told me they are working on papers for your Court Martial."

"What the hell for?" Carl asked in the dark.

"They've had some hot-shot CID investigator following you -- when you go out of camp in Sergeant Bowman's Chevy.

"I was going to wait until tomorrow to tell you -- so you would quit going out. They don't like your being in Bamberg after hours -- with that crowd from the Enlisted Men's Club -- that all night stuff."

"No crap," Carl said, sitting up in the dark.

He felt as if someone had just punched him in the face.

"The Army's been watching you for some time, the clerk said. All the way back to that escapade, where the lawyer got Lasslett off the hook at his first Court Martial."

"Why'd the clerk tell you this?" Carl asked in the dark, laying back on the bed, feeling his stomach go tight.

"He told me later, the same investigator reported his girlfriend to the German cops. She used cocaine -- and sold it sometimes. He wants to get even -- I guess. The clerk types up all this stuff -- that comes in during investigations. He types the investigation reports."

"Did he say when the Court Martial papers were going to be dropped on me?" Carl asked, reaching under the bed for the cognac bottle, feeling his heart pumping hard.

"He didn't know for sure, Carl. I just told you all I know -- so you could quit doing that all-night stuff in town."

Carl was sipping cognac, when the lights went on again.

"I've got to tap a kidney," Flannery said going to the door, barefoot.

*   *   *   *   *

The next morning at eight-thirty, the barracks door opened. When the light came on, Carl saw the cluster of chevrons on the sleeve of a field jacket; it was the First Sergeant from the Regimental Headquarters Company.

"We just got back from a three-day pass," Flannery said, throwing off his blanket, putting his feet on the floor. "We got back -- real late," he said to explain being in bed.

"You two are being moved back to the Headquarters Company barracks. There's room now. So pack your equipment," said the Sergeant, looking around the room, holding the door open, "and move over today -- after duty hours."

The Sergeant spoke in a matter-of-fact manner, Carl noticed, as if he already knew the two of them would be in bed, instead of typing at their desks.

"Right, Sergeant," Carl said getting out of bed, "we'll get right on it."

97

"Private Breckles," the Master Sergeant said looking at Carl calmly, "you are to sweep and mop the Headquarters barracks hall -- every day before you have breakfast and report for your duties at Regimental Headquarters. And you will wear a Class-A uniform and tie -- every day, Breckles, and you too Flannery."

Flannery made a face at Carl, opening his eyes wide, as the Sergeant pulled the door closed behind him.

"Class-A uniform," Carl said taking his wool pants on a hanger, out of the upright locker, "I wonder why we got to dress like we're going to be in a parade."

"To face a firing squad," Flannery said. "They never shoot a man wearing fatigues."

"Probably," Carl said. He bent down and took the cognac bottle out of the AWOL bag, and drank what remained in the bottle. "But today, the firing squad will have to wait -- because I'm going on Sick Call this morning."

"How come?" Flannery said. "You probably only got a bad hangover."

"No, no, Sluggo," Carl said pulling on his shirt, "It's more than a hangover -- I'm a sick man -- and it's not getting better. And somehow I've got to convince the Army doctors."

Flannery was pulling on a clean t-shirt, when he said, "You still think you have that consumption?"

After putting the cognac bottle back in the AWOL bag, Carl turned and sat down on his cot for a moment, holding his hands on his face.

"Yeah, I think I have TB -- but right now I need a drink more than anything. I feel like a -- wet washrag -- limp."

"I got a half-bottle of wine," Flannery said, pulling on his wool uniform pants.

"No kidding?" Carl said looking up at him. "Where is it? I'm really suffering today."

Flannery reached into his suitcase in the upright locker, and took out the small bottle.

"I won't throw it," he said holding it out.

Carl stepped across the tile floor, quickly, in his bare feet.

"Riesling?" Carl said. "Who drinks Riesling -- voluntarily? It's really sour."

He went back to his cot, found the AWOL bag, looking for his Army utility knife with the corkscrew.

"At Strasbourg," Flannery said, tying his shoe, sitting on his cot, "the tour bus from Paris stopped for lunch. The tables were already set -- and at each plate there was a half-bottle of Riesling."

Carl did not say anything while pulling the cork, then taking a sip of wine.

"Wh-hew," he said after swallowing.

"Sour, huh?" Flannery said. "But it's alcohol."

"Yeah, thanks," Carl said, before taking another sip.

"No, you should thank the lady," Flannery said while putting his tie through his shirt collar in back, "who didn't drink her Riesling.

"When she walked out of the café, I snitched her bottle off the table."

"She's a real humanitarian," Carl said forcing the cork back into the small bottle. "And she'll never know it."

CHAPTER 15

Carl and Flannery walked into the G-3 office later that morning, and as they were going to their desks, Lieutenant Taylor came out of the Adjutant's Office.

"Private Breckles," he said to Carl, "you are to report to the Dispensary this morning. There was a phone message from the Nuremberg Hospital. They requested you be sent there immediately -- for medical reasons."

"Yes, Sir. I'll catch the morning bus," Carl said, a sense of relief coming over him that something was going to be done about his chest pains.

"Hope you didn't catch something from the <u>shatzies</u> in town, Private."

"I hope not too, Sir," Carl said, as the Lieutenant turned to go into the Colonel's Office, grinning.

Flannery walked over to his desk and sat down, Carl standing, pulling down on his Eisenhower jacket in front, "Well," Carl said quietly, "I'm pretty sure what I got -- and now the Army knows it too -- and I feel like I just shot myself in the foot."

"Ah-h, it can't be that bad, Carl. Wait and see."

"Let's hope it's not too bad," Carl said putting on his narrow Overseas cap. "I'm going to the Dispensary."

"Good luck, Carl."

Walking to the Dispensary, Carl saw Sergeant Bowman's Chevrolet parked outside the Enlisted Men's Club.

"No more of that," he said to himself. "No more after hours trips to Bamberg for drinking with Bowman and that crowd."

After he said it, the thought came to him; Sergeant Bowman once said he was CID -- the Criminal Investigation Division of the Military Police.

"He could have been the one who turned in that report, about me going into Bamberg at night." Carl said, walking toward the Dispensary. "The son-of-a bitch -- was setting me up for a Court Martial."

"Naw," Carl said, "that can't be. Nobody would do something like that."

At the Dispensary, an orderly took Carl to a side room, turning on the light, pointing to a chair.

"The doctor will talk to you in a minute," the orderly said from the doorway. "He just came in."

Carl wondered why he was in this room. The examination rooms were across the hall.

He sat looking, elbows on his knees, at the scale in the room, the glass cabinets stacked with drug bottles, and the color chart of a body on the wall, showing in a cut-away picture of the heart and other internal organs.

When the door opened suddenly, the German doctor, wearing a paper mask covering his mouth and nose, came in, and to Carl, he looked like a stage coach robber, his black hair combed back, and the mask.

"Your x-rays were read in Nuremberg Hospital," the doctor said calmly, "and they want you to report there for further testing."

"Okay," Carl said. "They think I got Tuberculosis, don't they doctor?"

"This is not for certain," the doctor said. "But as a caution -- you must wear a paper mask -- at all times."

The doctor handed Carl a paper mask, taking it from a box on the cabinet.

"I'll put it on," Carl said, "when I get on the bus."

"No," the doctor said, putting both hands in the pockets of his white laboratory coat, "you are required to put the mask on now.

"And on the bus, you will restrict yourself to the rear section -- away from the other persons riding -- isolated. The driver will be informed."

Carl nodded, then put the mask on his face.

"Can I go get my shaving kit from the barracks?" Carl asked.

"No," the doctor said opening the door, "your personal belongings will be sent to you in Nuremberg. The bus leaves for there now, in twenty minutes."

Carl shrugged.

"You were correct in asking about the shadows that appeared on your previous x-ray," the doctor said slowly.

"Yes," Carl said moving the mask on his face to make it comfortable as he spoke, "but it doesn't make me feel better -- because I was right."

The doctor went out the door and closed it, not saying anything.

On the bus to Nuremberg, four seats in front of Carl was Private Whitaker, sitting with an MP guard.

Carl heard the story of the Whitaker fight. About how Whitaker had been in a nightclub with a shatz who got up and left him at the table. He was drunk, and staggered outside, looking for her. When he saw a woman at a bus stop, he grabbed her, and when she screamed, the Bamberg police came.

In the fight that followed, barrack's rumors in Fox Company had it that Whitaker's eye came out of the socket.

The woman at the bus stop was a schoolteacher.

Carl sat looking at Whitaker's face bandaged, remembering him from Basic Training at Fort Riley. He was a sheepherder from someplace in Montana.

It would be a long time before Whitaker sees Montana again, Carl thought. Damn, the same goes for me too; I'm not sure how long it takes to cure a lung disease.

At the hospital in Nuremberg, Carl was assigned to a bed in the Physical Rehabilitation Section, a Clinic, due to overcrowding.

Carl asked the orderly leading him to the room, why the hospital was so crowded.

"Some Battalion of Engineers from Erlangen came down with hepatitis," the orderly said as they were walking in a hallway. "We got almost a whole Company here -- they filled up most of the beds. I hear more are coming, too."

"What's hepatitis?" Carl asked, walking next to the orderly.

"A disease of the liver -- like an infection."

"How do you catch it? I mean so many guys."

"Maybe something in the water," the orderly said, shrugging.

"A whole Company," Cal said. "Maybe it was sabotaged."

"Could be," the orderly said. "Who knows."

"You mean I'm going to stay here -- in this hepatitis epidemic," Carl asked.

"They're starting to send the bad-off patients to the big Army Hospital in Frankfurt, I hear," the orderly said.

"Frankfurt?"

"Yeah," the orderly said, looking at room numbers, "we're really jammed up here."

"Frankfurt is three-hundred kilometers away from here," Carl said, and stopped walking.

"Yeah," the orderly said.

The next morning, Carl climbed on the bus with the patients selected to be sent to Frankfurt, wondering if their disease was contagious.

He saw the patients look at his facemask, and when no one sat near him, Carl realized they were wondering the same about him; if he had a contagious disease.

At the large Army Hospital in Frankfort, Carl changed his uniform in for pajamas and a robe, and was assigned a room in a remote part of the building.

"Feels like I'm in the Tower of London," he said to himself, lying on the bed in the room furnished with a single chair. "Talk about isolation -- I'm in it, that's for sure."

There was no television, and he could hear no activity out in the hall, like at the other hospitals he had been in. No one came to the room, except the orderly in a paper mask, who set his lunch tray on the chair.

But he did feel relief at being able to lay down, after all the bus travel. He was tired, and wanted to sleep.

Before closing his eyes, he wished the room had a window, so he could at least look out over the city of Frankfort.

After an orderly woke him, bringing the supper tray, he knew it was late in the day. He sat on the bed eating from the tray on his lap, and when the orderly returned for the tray, he was going to ask him for a cigarette.

But, before he could speak, the door opened slowly, and Carl saw a doctor with a white coat over his uniform and Colonel eagles on his shirt collar come into the room.

The orderly left with the tray, closing the door, after stepping around the Colonel, who began reading from the folder he carried.

"Private Carl Breckles?"

"Yes, Sir," Carl said sitting up straighter on the bed, his legs hanging over the edge.

"I'm doctor Eddington," the Colonel said, closing the folder in his hands. "I'm the hospital administrator, and I'm sorry we had to put you in this room -- but we have no isolation ward for your type of disease."

"I understand, Sir."

"I've been to Radiology looking at your x-rays," the Colonel said slowly, "and yours appears to be an advanced case of Tuberculosis. If you would have come a few months later -- we could not have done anything for you. It's not understandable that this disease was not discovered before now."

"Wow, Colonel. I tired to tell them at the Dispensary in Bamberg I had the disease, but they said different."

"There are drugs today," the Colonel said, as if not hearing Carl's comment about the Dispensary, "that will calcify the tuber lesions in your lung -- we call them P.A.S. and I.N.H for short."

"I'm glad to hear that, Colonel."

"We will start you on medication today," the Colonel said. "I will send the nurse back here with the pills for today. You will continue taking them as long as you are here -- three times a day with meals."

"Yes, Sir," Carl said, feeling gratified that his health problem was finally recognized, and being corrected.

He watched as the Colonel was writing in the open folder.

"You won't be here more than a few days," the Colonel said, looking up, closing the folder. "We are not a long-term care facility here. You will be sent to the United States for treatment -- on the first available medical air flight."

Opening the folder again, the doctor said, "I see you are from Michigan, so that means you will probably be sent to Valley Forge Army Hospital in Pennsylvania. It is the closest one near your home state."

"Yes, Sir. That will be fine, Sir."

"If you have any medical problem," the doctor said, lowering the folder, holding it at his side, moving to the door, "ring that buzzer on the bell cord, there at the head of your bed. The nurse will assist you.

"Again, I must say, bear with us on these room conditions. They won't last more than a day or two."

"Thank you, doctor," Carl said as the Colonel went out the door, thankful he was more doctor than Colonel.

Three days later, after eating lunch sitting on the bed, Carl decided to shave instead of taking a nap.

He unwrapped the throwaway plastic razor that came with a toothbrush and small bar of soap, rolled in a towel the nurse had given him.

He felt he was a prisoner; the single chair next to the small washbasin, thinking his room looked like photos of prison cells he had seen in magazines.

Looking in the wall mirror at the stubble on his face, he began lathering, thinking about whoever they sent from Headquarters Company supply room to collect his belongings, would help himself to his personal stuff, not to mention all his army issued field equipment.

He smiled, thinking about the barracks trick to open the wood, upright wall locker. He had seen it done.

There was a combination lock on the two-door locker, but you could open the doors with a helmet, turned upside down, putting the back of the helmet lip under the floor edge of the doors, stepping on the visor lip. The helmet rocked like a lever, and lifted both doors off the hinge pins, and would fall open.

Shaving his chin, looking in the mirror at the dark circles under his eyes, he suddenly felt a sense of gravity at being sick with TB. He realized, he could die from the disease. It was a possibility.

He stopped shaving, when the thought came to him, that he was out of the army too. They cannot Court Martial a sick man on his bed; they had no power over him anymore.

He was out of the army, and going home. He had not realized it before, what being an invalid meant.

He started shaving again, making a face at himself in the mirror, thinking he would do everything now to beat this disease. He would do everything they told him to do.

After dousing his face with cold water, he stretched out on the bed, his hands behind his head on the pillow.

"It's hard to believe," Carl said out loud slowly, "but this disease has changed -- everything. I never thought of that before."

There was a tapping at the door.

"Who is it?" Carl asked, knowing the doctors and nurses never knocked.

Margerite came into the room, a mask over her face, holding her oversized floppy hat with both hands.

"Carl," she softly, "I must talk with you."

"How did you get in here?" he asked, shocked at seeing her again, then feeling apprehension suddenly; he sensed she wanted something from him, but he could not imagine what.

"I told the nurse," Margerite said, laying her big hat on the end of the bed, "you must sign a business paper -- I am your business partner. If you go to the States, you must sign before you go."

"And the nurse let you come up here?"

"No, an orderly did. She heard me talking with the nurse. I gave the orderly woman -- forty Marks."

Margerite took off her raincoat and laid it on the bed next to her hat.

"That's only ten bucks, American," Carl said grinning, sitting up on the bed, cross-legged, as she came closer.

Margerite pulled down her mask, saying, "To some people that is a lot of money," then kissed Carl.

Her manner had a hard edge; maybe it was her business face she was showing, Carl thought looking at her. Or, she wanted something.

"You are not the only one -- with a medical problem, Carl," she said sitting on the edge of the bed, her perfume rising from her. "Sergeant Bowman -- had -- how do you say -- brain attack. At the Club -- two nights back. A blood clot.

"His face was purple -- and I heard -- he has -- some paralysis. The Army rushed him to Nuremberg, I heard."

"You came here on the train to tell me this?" Carl said, not wanting to show any satisfaction about Bowman and his cerebral hemorrhage.

"No, no, liebchen," she said. "I came to see you -- after Flannery told me at the Club he packed your things at the barracks to -- be sent here to Frankfort."

She slid off the bed to stand, opening her oversized purse, and took out a long box wrapped in silver foil.

"These are for you," she said, handing him the box. "I bought them here in Frankfort -- near the parking station. I have Victor's Volkswagen bus. They are chocolates -- filled with -- cognac inside."

"Hey, that's terrific," Carl said unwrapping one end of the box, opening it, taking out one of the chocolates, shaped like a small bottle and putting it in his mouth.

"Um-m," he said chewing, then grinning. "You are a wonder"

"I have business -- partners -- here in Frankfort. I can stay with them -- for a few days."

Carl reached for her, and standing up, pulled her to kiss her.

"Not just now," she said, putting both her hands on his chest. "I have come to ask -- if you have thought more about what I -- suggested -- in Munich?"

Carl, stood hesitant, looking at her.

"What are you talking about?"

"About taking me -- and my daughter -- to the States, lover," she said calmly. "We talked about this -- in Munich."

Carl looked at her, stunned by her question, feeling as if someone hit him in the back of his head. He stood looking at her face, the mask low hanging around her neck, feeling <u>his</u> face going red, and said, "But I'm going to the US on a stretcher -- a medical flight."

"Yes," Margerite said calmly, "but we could be married, and you could -- send for us."

Carl thought of saying something about her sanity, but restraining himself, said, "I have a serious disease -- it's taking all my attention -- all my energy -- to get over it."

"Carl," she said putting her hand to the side of his face, "I am -- desperate -- to get to the United States."

He was going to make a wisecrack, that half the girls in Europe all wanted to go to the land of the big PX.

"There is nothing I can do," Carl said, trying to restrain himself. "The army is running my life, right now, and they are taking me home."

He thought if he said this enough, he could avoid a direct refusal.

"You mean, Carl, you will not take me to the States?"

"It's out of my hands -- completely, Margerite."

She pulled away from him, and in a low voice, said, "You are a bastard. I come all this way -- now you tell me this."

"I have no choice, Margerite. You understand I'm in the army," he said, to thwart her request, and let her down easy, at the same time. "If things were different, maybe --"

"You do not want to marry me," she said, turning away from him, going to the end of the bed.

"I can't," Carl said, blinking.

There was a silence, as Margerite picked up her coat and hat off the bed.

"You and Sergeant Bowman -- have what you -- deserve. Both of you," she said walking to the door, holding her coat and hat.

"The Sergeant told me the military police -- they want to put you in the army prison -- and I was -- about to tell you this. Now you both," she said pulling on her raincoat, "are both destroyed."

When she closed the door, Carl saw the mask she wore lying on the floor where she dropped it.

Carl sat down on the bed, taking another chocolate cognac candy out of the box, putting it in his mouth, he grinned, shaking his head.

The nurse came into the room, wearing a mask.

"Medication time," she said, her cart stacked with other patient medications, showing in the doorway. She was holding two paper cups, all the pills Carl had to take.

"Could you get me some writing paper?" Carl asked her, spilling the near handful of PAS tablets into his hand from the cup. "I want to write home -- tell my parents I'm coming to the US."

"No need," the nurse who wore Captain bars, said. "The Red Cross will send a telegram to them. They always do."

Carl took one half of the pills with water, sitting on the bed. It was an effort to swallow so many, but he did. Then the remainder pills went into his mouth, and he drank all the water in the glass to get them down.

"Just the same, Mam, would you bring me some writing paper?"

She had stood, watching him swallow the pills, and when she turned to go to the door, stooping to pick up the mask Margerite dropped, "All right," she said. "By the way -- you are scheduled for a medical flight home in two days, I hear. You'll probably be in the US before the letter."

CHAPTER 16

It was late afternoon of the day Carl had been operated on at the VA Hospital, having the infected part of his lung removed.

He had only been conscious for minutes, a post operation nurse watching him, a small suction pump running on the floor next to his bed.

"What's that thing on television?" he asked weakly.

The post-op nurse was sitting in a chair at the foot of the bed. She was watching the television set on the opposite wall, showing what looked like a ball with several antenna protruding.

"Sputnik," the nurse said, getting up, bending to check the two drain hoses coming out of Carl's chest, attached to the pump on the floor. "It's a satellite -- the Russians shot up in space today. It is circling the earth. Everybody around the world is watching it on television."

"No kidding?" Carl said, watching as the nurse lifted the sheet, checking the side of his chest where the tubes went in, taped to his ribs.

Carl did not feel pain, the Demerol drug still working to keep him numb, light-headed. But it burned, when he moved, particularly the eight-inch incision under his should blade, where the doctors went in to remove the part of his lung.

So Carl lay still.

Looking at the television set again, "Guess the Russians are way ahead of us," he said to the nurse. "They are out there in space -- first."

The nurse was lifting the clear jug, half-filled with water, that the pump was emptying into; there were streaks of blood in the water, Carl could see.

"We'll catch-up with them," the nurse said, setting it back down. "You can bet on that."

Carl watched as she wrote on a clipboard paper. Feeling drowsy, he drifted to sleep, feeling relief. He had entered the operating room at seven this morning, and had just woke up now. All the tension, and worry, was behind him, the Sputnik making the day easy to remember.

*   *   *   *   *

Carl had been getting out of bed after a month, going only to the Physical Therapy sessions; he was told to strengthen the shoulder muscles to keep them from dropping, particularly on the side of the operation.

He was growing restless, and on the evening after dinner, when he saw other patients passing in the hall, walking in their bathrobes, going down to the movie in the hospital auditorium, he followed.

Standing in the elevator from the third floor, going down to the Main Floor of the hospital, dressed in his bathrobe and paper slippers, he asked the patient next to him, "Hey, what's showing tonight?"

"That Kim Novak -- in <u>Picnic</u>," the patient said. "Everybody's going to see her."

Downstairs in the auditorium, Carl took an end seat, and by leaning to his right, he kept his body weight away from straining the operation on his left shoulder.

When the theater lights dimmed, Carl smiled, feeling the relief of having gotten away from the ward, and gotten away with it.

Suddenly, the theater lights came back on.

A voice on the loudspeaker system said to the auditorium, "Will patient Carl Breckles return to Ward 3-B immediately. The movie for tonight will not begin until he does so."

Carl hesitated for almost a minute, listening to the murmuring of the crowd.

Relenting, he stood up, and began walking slowly up the incline of the aisle to the back theater door.

Clapping started, sporadic at first, then the whole auditorium joining in as he shuffled up to the door.

In the elevator going back up to the third floor, he smiled, wondering if the theater audience was clapping for his attempt to escape the ward for a while, or simply because he did not hold up the movie from being show.

Three months after the operation on his chest, Carl was told he could go home for the Christmas Holidays.

He felt he had been an invalid long enough, and after Christmas did not return to the Veteran's Hospital. He walked as much as possible, despite the snow, and ignored the letters, and even phone calls from fellow patients, telling him he should return.

A month later he received a letter from the VA hospital, stating his official status was "leaving the hospital -- against medical advice."

He was living at home, trying to make himself useful around the house, doing errands for his mother.

It was a Tuesday afternoon. He came home, opening the back kitchen door carrying two shopping bags, stamping the snow off his shoes.

In the kitchen he shouted to his mother sitting at the table in the dining room, "The snow is really coming down. The roads are getting clogged -- dad will be getting home late for dinner."

He could see his mother through the doorway; she was opening Christmas cards, and had them spread out on the table.

"I hope the girls will be all right," his mother said, while opening one of the cards.

"Those two are always 'all right,'" Carl said to ease her mind.

His two sisters, Carol and Theresa, eleven and nine years old, dominated the activities at their Anthony Wayne Grammar School. They joined most of the school programs, and Carl knew it. He knew his mother knew it too.

"I didn't get a card from the Maxwell's this year," Carl heard his mother say. "I'm not going to send them a card, next year."

"Hey, Mom, that's not the Christmas spirit," Carl said, lifting a large pack of frozen chicken from the shopping bag, then opening the freezer compartment of the refrigerator, and setting it inside.

"I couldn't get the small pack of chicken," he said, closing the freezer door, "so I bought the sixty-four ounce size. I saved forty-cents, Mom."

"Son," his mother said back through the open doorway, "how can you save money -- by spending more?"

"That's a good question, Mom," Carl said, putting two Cheerio boxes up in a cabinet, grinning.

"Oh, son, there's a card for you here in the mail -- it's from Wisconsin. I didn't open it."

"No kidding?" Carl said, walking through the doorway, taking the envelope from her hand.

"O-oh," his mother said, looking across the table, seeing the blowing snow through the large windows, "it's really coming down heavy."

She looked up at Carl, "Now don't you go out there and try shoveling, son. It's too soon -- you're just out of the hospital."

"No, I won't shovel, Mom," he said, looking at the Christmas card in his hand, addressed in green ink, a woman's handwriting.

"And no pushing cars that get stuck," his mother said sorting through the cards again. "Promise me."

"I promise," he said putting the card in his teeth, pulling off his quilted jacket, wondering if she knew about his leaving the Veteran's Hospital "against medical advice."

"Father understands," his mother said picking up another card. "We talked about your condition."

"O-oh," she said suddenly, "the Coleman's sent us a card this year -- and I didn't send them one."

Carl walked back to the kitchen, hung his jacket on a hook near the back door, and sat down in the breakfast nook, looking at the card.

Using a butter knife, he opened the envelope, not sure Jackie Lasslett sent it.

Flipping open the card, showing a snowman wearing a Santa cap, the inside read a non-committal "Holiday Greetings," but on the back was a note.

> We had an easy flight from Frankfort to
> Chicago. Martha slept most of the way.
> Thinking now I should bring Mike home
> for burial here in Wisconsin. Hope everything
> is okay with your health.
>   Jackie Lasslett

Carl looked up, when his mother walked through the doorway into the kitchen.

"Is that a card from one of your girlfriends?" she asked smiling.

"No, Mom, it's from an army buddy."

"That's a girl's handwriting," his mother said calmly while lifting two cans of peaches out of the shopping bag, setting them on a shelf over the sink. "You're not keeping her a secret, are you?"

"No, my buddy's wife sends out their cards at Christmas," Carl said while sliding the card back in the envelope.

He sat for a moment, looking at the handwriting, wondering how Jackie <u>did</u> get his home address.

Maybe, he thought, Lasslett simply saw him writing the address on a letter home, sitting in the PX cafeteria back at Fort Riley.

"I'm going to make cabbage rolls for supper tonight," his mother said opening the freezer door, then taking out the frozen meat-rolls in a flat plastic container. "Go downstairs to the cellar, and bring up a jar of applesauce for me."

"Is that all?" Carl asked, getting up from the table.

"See if there's a jar of dill pickles left," she said slamming the freezer door.

"Okay."

Going down the back stairs to the basement, snapping on the light, Carl said to himself, "Jackie -- 'let the sleeping dog -- lie.' Leave him be -- in peace."

When he came back upstairs, Carl set the jars of applesauce and pickles on the counter, next to where his mother was slicing a banana cake.

"Is there a card no one has written on?"

"If you want a card," his mother said while laying the cake slices on a circular platter, "I'll give you a <u>new</u> one -- don't be so cheap." She followed him, wiping her hands.

"Okay," Carl said smiling, walking to the dining room table, and sitting down.

"Here," his mother said, selecting a card. "And here's a stamp too. Now let me get dinner ready; no more interruptions, son."

Carl sat looking at the return address on the card from Jackie.

"Lacrosse Wisconsin," he said. "Maybe she's just feeling guilty, or something, for leaving Lasslett over in Europe."

He began writing Jackie Lasslett's address, when it hit him: "This card is -- bait," he said quietly. "She wants me to contact her -- what would she gain bringing Lasslett back to the US?"

He leaned back in the chair, thinking, Jackie knows, I would say to leave Lasslett buried where he is.

So he wrote:

> Glad to hear you both back at the
> ranch -- safe and sound.
>   Carl

"Do they have any children?" Carl's mother asked from the kitchen. "This army buddy and his wife?"

"Yes, a little girl," Carl said sliding the card into the envelope, watching the nativity scene disappear, except for the star that still shone down from the corner.

"How did you ever meet up with them?"

"During Basic Training -- I knew him from the barracks at Fort Riley in Kansas," he said, wetting his thumb, running it on the envelope glue.

He wrote the address, beginning with Mrs. Jackie Lasslett.

"Did the -- wife and baby come to Germany?"

"Yes," Carl said, glancing at the snow falling, now in large flakes; it made him think of how damp the weather was in Germany. "But we were in different barracks -- over seas -- I didn't see him much."

"How did you become such good friends?" his mother asked, after making a loud <u>ping</u> in the kitchen when setting the metal Dutch oven on the stove. "You must have spent time with them -- to rate a Christmas card."

"Yes," Carl said, shaking his head, listening to her barrage of questions, still watching the snow. "He had some legal trouble, and I knew another soldier who was a lawyer -- who helped him out."

"And the wife wrote you a Christmas card for that?" his mother's voice coming in an inquisitive tone. "How come?"

"Maybe they think they owe me something," Carl said, standing up, pushing the dining room chair under the table.

Carl stood holding the card and realized he could not let his mother see that it was addressed to Jackie.

He decided he could hide the card in his college books and mail it on the way to night classes at the University tomorrow.

Carl heard the kitchen backdoor open, and the loud talking as the two sisters came in from school, slamming the door.

Carl walked to his bedroom, and seeing his history book on the desk, slipped the card between the pages.

*   *   *   *   *

Eleven days later, Carl came home from night classes at Wayne University, when his mother whispered from her television chair in the living room, over his father napping in the next chair, "There are two letters for you on the dining table."

"Thanks," Carl whispered back.

"One is from the Department of the Army," she whispered without turning around. "The other has that girl's handwriting."

Carl felt his mouth drop open, as he turned slowly, pulling off his quilted jacket, then the heavy wool sweater he wore against the bitter-cold weather outside.

He walked out to the kitchen, snapped on the overhead light, carrying the two letters, looking at them while hanging his coat on a peg, flinging the sweater on a chair.

The Department of the Army letter was a coarse tan envelope, and Jackie's was smaller, not even the size of her Christmas card.

"Is that letter from the same woman -- who sent the card?" his mother said, coming into the kitchen, startling him for a moment.

She was carrying an empty popcorn bowl, and he saw burnt kernels on the bottom.

"I think so," Carl said.

"You said she's the <u>wife</u> -- of your army buddy," his mother said coolly, as she dumped the unpopped kernels in the trash bucket under the sink. "She's married -- isn't she?"

"Something might have happened," Carl said to blunt her questions.

"Or," his mother said, filling the bowl with bought popcorn from a bag the size of a pillow, "maybe something is <u>about</u> to happen."

"You're missing the Lawrence Welk program, Mom," he said, hoping to distract her.

It was her favorite television program, and while she watched, his father took a nap, uninterested.

"Be careful, son," his mother said, putting two large paperclips on the folded top of the popcorn bag to seal it. "Don't get into something with that girl -- she has a child, and you are not strong enough to take on responsibilities, a job -- not yet."

"Where are the girls?" he said as if he knew it too, but wanted to change the subject.

"They're practicing swimming at the school pool," his mother said putting the popcorn bag on a shelf in the closet. "They want to be ready for the girl's swim team -- when they get to high school."

Walking to the kitchen door, his mother, carrying the bowl of popcorn, said, "I just want you to be careful -- you're not fully recovered from what they did at the hospital."

"I know what you mean, Mom," Carl said looking at the small envelope he had opened.

When his mother went out of the kitchen, he pulled the letter out of an envelope, and unfolding it, saw it was written on business paper, the emblem of a cow and a fence at the top, and the name, Boulanger Dairy Farm.

> Carl, will you help me with some legal
> stuff, like you helped Mike?
> I went to the Veteran's Administration,
> but they said they could not help.
> They gave me your address, and I sent
> you the Christmas card.
> I want to ask if you know any legal
> stuff that might help me bring Mike
> home to be buried here in Wisconsin.
> Jackie

CHAPTER 17

Carl sat looking at Jackie's letter for a moment, then slowly slid it back into the envelope.

"Wow," he said to himself, "she really knows how to put a guy on the spot. I'm not that good with legal moves. It was just luck -- I knew that lawyer back in the PX at Bamberg." He put Jackie's letter aside.

Picking up the Department of the Army envelope, he opened it, and read through it twice.

The Army sent notice that after a medical evaluation, Carl would be Honorably Discharged, since his enlistment time was served, and he was to turn in his AGO card, his military identification.

After a medical exam, the information would be sent to Fitzsimmons Army Hospital in Denver, Colorado. The exam would determine how much disability pension Carl would receive by an Army board of doctors at Fitzsimmons.

The nearest military hospital, where Carl was to report for the medical exam, was the Great Lakes Naval Training Facility at Milwaukee, Wisconsin.

Carl's home in Detroit was located in the Fifth Army Headquarters district in Chicago, and the nearest military hospital in the area was the naval one. So he was to report there.

"I'm in the Army," Carl said putting the Army letter back in the envelope, "so they send me to the <u>Navy</u> for a physical."

He shook his head, grinning, saying, "That figures."

Looking at the two letters coming at the same time.

"I wonder how far LaCross, Wisconsin is -- from Milwaukee?"

His mother came back into the kitchen, and opened the refrigerator door. She took out an orange juice carton.

"You were talking to yourself," she said, while pouring the orange juice into a small glass.

"I'm just grumbling," he said. "The letter from the Army says they want me to report to Milwaukee -- for a medical exam."

"Oh, I see," she said putting the carton back in the refrigerator. "You don't want to go?"

"It's a long trip -- just to take an x-ray," he said, looking at Jackie's letter, thinking he should send her a note, telling her when he could be in Milwaukee.

"Doris?" his father shouted from the living room, "bring me a Budweiser when you come back."

* * * * *

That spring, Carl drove his five-year old Ford to Milwaukee for an April fourteenth scheduled medical exam.

He bought the four-door Ford with its stick shift, for five hundred dollars he saved while in the Veterans Hospital. He liked this year Ford; he had memories.

It reminded him of a fun trip to Saugatuck, when he and a girl drove to the beach parties in the summer colony. It was the girl's father's car, a second car the family had. They had a lot of money. He remembered how he liked driving it, when he spelled her at the wheel during the long trip.

When he spotted this car on a used car lot, he bought it.

Now the Army was paying six cents a mile for driving from Detroit to Milwaukee.

But, more than that, travelling again, gave him a twinge of excitement, like he had in the days before he went into the Army. And here he was, getting out.

At Milwaukee, he was given a bed in the nearly empty hospital of the Naval base. There were no other patients in his room.

"We won't give you dinner," the orderly in a blue sailor suit said to Carl. "We want to check the overnight drainage in your stomach in the morning -- the sputum check.

"You'll be given breakfast after blood is drawn, and you have chest x-rays. Then you will be free to go."

Carl nodded saying, "Cripe -- that's the same bunch of tests they do at the Veterans Hospital -- where I go every three months for follow-up exams," he said, in protest for his coming all this way.

"Then you know the drill," the orderly said, pushing his eyeglasses up on his nose higher. "We'll start the tests -- just after six tomorrow morning."

"I'll be here," Carl said to the orderly going out the room door.

Lying on the bed in pajamas, Carl was watching the television showing the movie How The West Was Won, when he began thinking of Jackie, and wishing now he had answered her letter.

He had started, twice, to write her, but tore up the paper, reasoning it was not his place to get involved.

He had to admit to himself, when Lasslett was Court Martialed the second time, he deliberately avoided helping. He wanted to save his own skin. Later he had a vague impression the army was working to put him behind bars too.

But now, he began to feel guilt for not helping Jackie. It was as if he felt guilty for Lasslett hanging himself, and now, when his widow was asking for help, he was doing nothing again.

He told himself, get away from the whole thing. Stop thinking about it. Be smart about this.

But, her letter continued pressing on his thoughts. He began to reason, by helping her bring the body home, he could clear his conscience, and finalize the whole problem.

Being less than two hundred miles from Jackie's home, began running through his mind, everything seemed to be pushing him toward helping her.

When the movie ended, he slipped off the bed, and barefoot, walked over to snap off the television set.

Coming back to get on the bed, a thought crossed his mind.

"Hey," he said pulling the blanket up, "maybe I can talk her out of bringing the body back here. That would solve the whole thing, dummy."

He lay for a moment, thinking of Jackie, remembering when he last saw her in Bamberg, how she told him she was "lonely," and he smiled.

Maybe this whole thing about bringing the body back -- is just a trick -- to see if he would come to her.

He grinned in the dark, thinking, there is only one way to find out. Go see her, and all your questions will be answered.

* * * * *

After the tests, when he was released from the Naval hospital, Carl went to his car, where he took the roadmap out of the glove box, and sat studying it.

"La Crosse is about two hundred and fifty miles from here," he said, starting the car, shifting into first gear. "After Madison, it's only a couple inches on the map."

In late afternoon, passing through Madison, and driving now, beyond the state capitol, Carl felt the driving taking a tole on his strength, his energy level sinking.

"I should have just wrote Jackie a letter," he said driving, "I could have begged-off -- from helping her bring Lasslett home -- and been done with the whole thing."

But in the evening, driving into the city of La Crosse, seeing across the Mississippi River to Minnesota on the other side, he felt a rush. He was not sure if he felt the jolt from the travel adventure side of himself, or if it was the chance of seeing Jackie again. She was easy to look at.

In a flash, he saw his whole experience with her; the town of Bamberg, Germany, wet cobblestone streets, his being in the Army, Lasslett being in jail, his suicide, finding out about the Tuberculosis, but above all, how she was attracted to him.

Then it suddenly hit him. He was no longer bound by the taboo of not making a pass at a buddy's wife. Lasslett was gone. Jackie was a free woman.

"Wow," he said to himself, looking for a phone booth, "that was in the back of my head all this time -- but now it's out. Jackie can do what she chooses. And I hope she chooses me."

Grinning, he walked to the phone booth, and looking for the dairy farm number, leafing through the pages of the thick book, he looked up, saying "That was no Christmas card -- she sent me an invitation."

"Is that really you, Carl?" Jackie asked over the phone.

"Yep. I had to go to Milwaukee for an Army physical -- and I thought -- well, that I'd say hello."

"Milwaukee? Where are you now?"

"Here in La Crosse," he said, shifting his weight to one leg, standing in the booth. "I drove up to see you -- it was only a few inches on the map from Milwaukee -- but it turned out to be a little further than I expected."

"Oh-h," she said, a smile in her voice, "I'm so happy you came up. Really. We can talk -- I have to talk to you."

"Okay," he said, searching for something to say, and not sound too excited. "I didn't know -- what to write you back -- after I got your letter."

"Carl, you come out to the farm -- stay here. Okay?"

"Sure."

She gave him directions, and in the dark, he found the farm sign on the highway, and turning up the driveway, saw the long, low house, in the yard lights, and the barn behind, and the rail fences, painted white, that seemed to be everywhere on the property.

Jackie answered the door in tight denim pants and wearing moccasins.

She seemed much shorter, Carl thought, since he last saw her in Bamberg at the apartment.

"It's so good to see you, Carl. You remind me of the time -- of the things that happened with Mike in the Army."

"Well," he said feeling awkward, "maybe we should not remember the things that went on then -- I mean keep them in sort of proportion -- to the good things now."

Looking around at the comfortable furnishings of the living room, Carl could not help wondering why Jackie left all of this for Lasslett, who did not have two nickels to rub together.

Stepping further into the large living room, Carl saw a thin man, sitting at a desk at the far end, near a picture window, overlooking the farmyard behind.

Following Jackie to the desk, Carl saw the man wore a golf shirt, and despite his grey hair, looked fit, like an athlete.

"Daddy, this is Carl," Jackie said. "He was an army friend of Mike's. He's from Detroit."

"You drove up from Michigan?"

"Yesterday," Carl said. "I had an appointment in Milwaukee. I drove from there, today."

"Too bad it's dark," the father said in a friendly, business tone, "we could show you around the farm -- show you how it works."

"Maybe tomorrow, Daddy," Jackie said, taking hold of Carl's arm.

"I've never seen a dairy farm," Carl said, but before he could say more, followed Jackie, who was pulling his arm firmly.

"Nice meeting you," Carl heard the father say, as Jackie pulled him out of the living room into a hallway.

In the hall, they passed a room with a Ping-Pong table, and the sound of bouncing balls on a hard surface, and Carl caught a glimpse of two teenaged boys, playing.

A loud television set was showing a western movie.

"That's my brothers," Jackie said. "They're twins. I have an older sister -- who practically lives in the library in La Crosse. She's a researcher for the state Dairy Board."

Jackie had not spoken to the boys, but Carl noticed they saw him walking with her, and made faces at one another, as if they knew what she had planned.

When Jackie let go of his arm, Carl followed her into the kitchen, with a gaping brick fireplace, dark, at the far end, a modern stove, sink and refrigerator along the right wall, a long bar wood table with chairs down the center, and the entire left wall, all windows.

Carl had the impression this kitchen was well planned, well thought out.

"Where's your mom?" Carl asked, innocently.

"She's president of her Bridge Club," Jackie said, washing her hands at the sink. "They meet on Wednesdays -- tonight. She won't be home -- until late," Jackie said, drying her hands, looking at Carl, smiling.

"Nice home you have here," Carl said, sitting down on a chair next to the long table, as if exhausted by the home tour.

Looking out the windows, he could only see white fencing in the dark yard, showing in the lighting from the barn.

"I know," Jackie said smiling, her hand on her hip. "Would you like something to eat? Some eggs? How about coffee?"

"Coffee would be great," Carl said, unsure how he should act with Jackie.

"I'll scramble you some eggs, Carl. While the coffee perks," Jackie said, taking off her short jacket, hanging it on the chair next to Carl.

She moved, knowing Carl was watching her at the stove. Her narrow hips, and round bottom, filling out the tight denim pants, had his attention, she was sure.

"Okay if I sprinkle a little parsley on your eggs?" she asked from the stove, and turning suddenly, caught Carl looking at her bottom.

"Sure," Carl said, looking away, aware now that they both knew what the other was thinking.

"My mom has an herb garden out back," Jackie said, grinning, turning quickly back to stirring the eggs in the fry pan.

"Yeah," Carl said, "I've heard that parsley -- is -- healthy."

"If you want toast, Carl," she said turning around, a hand on her hip, "the breadbox is right behind you on the counter. So is the toaster," she said pointing with a wood spoon.

Leaning back, without getting up, and while dropping two slices of wheat bread in the toaster, Carl said slowly, "Your Christmas card said you were thinking of bringing Mike's body back from Europe."

He saw her mouth drop open for a moment, then close.

When she brought the frying pan over to the table, she said, like a school teacher to a pupil, "You don't think much of the plan, to bring him home? Do you?" she asked, pushing scrambled eggs onto his plate.

Carl looked up at her, not speaking.

"Neither does my dad -- only he says it would cost too much."

Carl sat looking at her standing next to him, her body seemingly saying, "take hold of me."

"Your toast is up, Carl."

He watched her set the frying pan back on the stove, then come to the table, and sit in the chair across from his, folding her arms.

"Okay," Carl said, feeling confident now, "I think you should leave him buried there in France."

Picking up a fork, looking at the flecks of green for a moment, he began eating the eggs.

"But -- I feel I owe him -- something," she said leaning forward, elbows on the table, hands together. "I mean it bothers me -- even though Martha was sick -- and I was busy -- he needed me, and I let him down.

"He must have felt -- I <u>deserted</u> him. Then he did that terrible thing -- to take his life."

"Jackie," Carl said, stopping his eating, but looking down at the eggs, "bringing him back here -- won't change anything. I mean -- it won't do him any good."

"But -- it will for me Carl. My conscience -- it's as if I deserted him <u>again</u> -- leaving him over there in France."

CHAPTER 18

"She seems awfully chubby," Carl whispered to Jackie.

"All babies -- are chubby;" she whispered back, closing the door softly, smiling, as they turned to walk up the hallway from Martha's room.

"And thank goodness -- she's healthy now."

"Right," Carl said, taking a deep breath. "Ah, I should be going," he said at the end of the hall, when they stopped walking.

"You came all this way, Carl -- to only tell me to leave Mike buried in France?"

"Yeah, I guess so," he said, looking at her face, as if trying to find a blemish.

"Maybe you don't know why you came here," Jackie said, putting her hands on his shoulders. "I know why."

He kissed her, and felt her pushing against him, hard.

"Mike saw how we looked at one another," Jackie said quietly, her face close to Carl's, "back in that dumb trailer at Fort Riley."

Carl's mouth opened, but he did not speak, looking straight at her eyes.

"He sent me to the room, when you went there to feed the baby -- I remember," he said slowly.

"I know," Jackie said. "He wanted to see -- what you would do."

Carl leaned back, thinking first in disbelief, then feeling a resentment toward Lasslett.

"You -- you knew this," he said, "all the time -- even back in Bamberg?"

He stood wondering if she was saying this as a trick to make him feel guilty for Lasslett hanging himself.

"Yes," she said. "He was so sure, he even bought me a gun. He was very jealous -- and protective. I still have the gun."

Carl let go of her, stepping back.

"Mike said I should use the gun -- if things got out of hand. I think he had you in mind, Carl."

"I think it's time for me to get going," he said, looking at the floor.

"Where are you going?"

"Just on the road -- La Crosse. Or maybe I'll drive until I get tired, and get a motel.

"I'm on an Army travel allowance -- I get mileage, and all that," he said, lying, to be convincing.

"You don't have to go, Carl. You can stay here."

"Naw," he said, rubbing his hand that had been in a cast, "I can't barge in on your family."

"You won't be," Jackie said taking hold of his hand. "We have a guest room."

"I don't want to impose on your folks, he said weakly, feeling Jackie's hand on his chest.

He kissed her, not wanting to let go.

"It's only a room over the garage," she said, smiling up at him, her hand on his face. "There's those double bunk beds. Sometimes dad hires guys to work on the farm -- they sleep there."

Carl smiled.

"I don't want --" be began.

"You won't be," she said, pulling his arm. "Come on, I'll show you." When she moved, he followed hearing her saying "Sometimes, even truck drivers bunk there -- they sleep over, and get an early start -- in the morning, when the cows are loaded."

"Naw, I can't stay," he said, stopping, looking at her.

"Don't be like that," Jackie said, taking his arm, pulling hard, "It's nothing fancy. There's no shower -- just a wash basin and a bippy."

Carl felt betrayed by Lasslett, when Jackie said that about him looking at her. Everybody looks at everybody else -- especially men, when it comes to women.

Carl began walking again, Jackie still holding his hand. He told himself, it was a mistake coming here.

"You got a girl?" Jackie asked. She was walking beside him now, looking up. "You got a girlfriend back in Detroit, Carl?"

"I'm going with -- a couple of girls," he said. "I meet a lot of girls -- in the classes I take."

"College girls," Jackie said, laughing. "They're a wild bunch." She stopped walking.

"They haven't got anything more -- than I have."

Before he could speak, she pressed up against him, her arms around his neck.

He tried to kiss her, but she dodged away.

"C'mon," she said pulling his arm, "let's go up to the bunk house."

As they were walking, arms around one another, Carl saw the barn in the distance was lit up brightly.

"Why all the lights?" Carl asked.

"That's dad," Jackie said, walking in step with Carl. "He's checking his cows."

Going up the steps at the bunkhouse, Carl, following Jackie, smelled the faint odor of disinfectant.

Neither of them spoke going through the door, and when he pulled her to kiss her again, he heard the zipper on her jacket go down.

"Here's a rubber," she whispered. "Medium size."

Pressing against him, Carl felt her moving her stomach in a slow rhythm.

Carl lowered her down on the bottom bunk, and sat next to her, feeling her lowering her tight denims; he started to lay himself out next to her.

"No," she whispered. "Do it from the back. Do it from the back -- like the animals do. It's too much -- these pants are too tight -- to pull off."

She raised up on her hands and knees, her face away from Carl.

He straddled her, the witness of her soft bottom, pushing against him, exciting to take hold of her hips, and wearing the prophylactic, he entered her.

"There," she whispered. "Oh-h, yes, there," she said pressing her face into the bunk mattress, raising her bottom higher. "Oh-h --"

She kept Carl excited more, by pushing her bottom back against him, and when the perspiration made her skin moist, he went into a frenzy, short strokes, until he climaxed.

"Don't stop," she said, when he was lying beside her on the bunk bed.

"Let me take this thing off," he said, dropping it on the floor.

"Give me more; forget the rubber. Just give me more -- we can't stop. Please don't stop. I need more.

"It's been a long time -- for me -- since I made love."

Carl did not feel tired, and with his heart pumping, he put his hands on her hips, raising her.

Suddenly, the room became bright, a light from outside the window coming from down on the ground below.

"What the hell's that light?" Carl snapped.

"My mother's car," Jackie whispered hoarsely, suddenly, going limp. "Damn," she said, laying herself flat on the mattress. "She's home from the Bridge Club."

Carl watched as Jackie, moving seductively from side to side, pulled up her tight pants.

While Carl was dressing, sitting on the edge of the bunk bed, Jackie put a hand on his neck.

"You -- you got to stay -- a couple of days, Carl," she said. "You <u>have</u> to stay. I need you."

"My finals at the university -- are only ten days away. The spring term is winding down. I've got to review --"

"Stay with me, Carl," Jackie said, getting off the bed. "I got nobody here. The guys stay away -- they don't want a woman with a child -- for a girlfriend."

Going down the steps from the bunk house, Carl said, "I'd like to stay here for a while, Jackie, but I owe my folks. They've been putting me up at home while I'm going to the university. I've got to do good in my classes."

"Common," Jackie said in a near pleading tone, "you can stay a day or two."

Carl, looking at her, trying to think of a good excuse for not staying, and at the same time, becoming aware, Jackie was not the person he thought she was.

"No, really," he said, "I should be heading back to Detroit. It's great you offered me the bunk house tonight, but I can't accept."

"You being here," Jackie said, pressing against him, "makes me remember the good times with Mike -- at Fort Riley, and over in Bamberg. And how happy I was."

"Well," Carl said, "you've got Martha to think about now. You can't live in the past, Jackie. You have a child."

Looking Carl in the face, stopping him from walking, as they were crossing the farmyard, she said, "I never told anybody this -- but -- I'm not sure Martha is Mike's baby."

"You're not just saying that?"

"No. It was just after I married Mike -- and he joined the army."

"You can't mean that," Carl said, squinting at her.

"When Mike went to jail here for stealing some tires, just after we were married," Jackie said, her head to one side, "I went out with a guy I knew from high school. He's the golf pro at the Golf Club here -- and he's married."

Carl felt like a fool for coming here.

"I should get going," he said, knowing it sounded clumsy.

But he felt now, Jackie was not the person he thought she was. She was cashing-in on his friendship with Lasslett, getting him here, now trying to make a permanent relationship.

All these things she was telling him, instead of making the two of them more intimate, was pushing him further away from her.

"C'mon, Carl, we can have a lot of fun -- while you're here," she said, putting a hand on the side of his face.

"Maybe next time," he said taking hold of the wrist of her hand on his face. "My classes -- are important."

"Screw your classes," she said, pursing her kips.

"Take it easy," he said, as she stepped back, looking at him. "We're not in Bamberg now."

"You make me think of Bamberg," she said, grinning, "in a way that's almost -- comical. When Mike was being Court Martialed, I was dating the head waiter at the Gablemann Café."

Carl was stunned but tried hard not to show any reaction to her remark.

He knew the waiter, Kurt, a young German guy, who was always making wisecracks in English. He acted as if he was going to be a millionaire someday, and was just waiting tables to fill time. The kind of guy who was full of himself, and had a high-opinion of himself.

One night at the Gablemann, Carl remembered sitting with Margerite and Sergeant Bowman, seeing a former Wehrmacht soldier, who had lived in Bamberg before the war and had just been released from a Russian prison camp, was sitting at the next table. He was one of the few prisoners of war who came home from the Eastern Front in World War II.

Kurt was making a fuss over the returned prisoner, serving him free expensive cognac, and the prisoner asked if he had a girl.

Carl remembered that Kurt said boastfully, he was going with the young wife of an American soldier. He said she had given him the cashmere scarf he wore around his neck.

The re-patriated German soldier smiled and nodded approval, before sipping the expensive cognac.

And Carl remembered Kurt took one end of the expensive scarf, and blew his nose in it. Carl was not sure if Kurt was showing contempt for the young, American wife, or maybe American's in general.

The ex-German soldier said nothing to Kurt, just poured another drink of expensive cognac from the bottle Kurt had brought to the table.

Carl thought now maybe Jackie was the young, American wife, but he said nothing.

He stood looking at her, remembering someone at the table in the Gablemann Café asked the soldier how long he had been in captivity.

He said he was seventeen when he was captured on the Eastern Front. That made him about thirty-five years old, and Carl, overhearing them talking, was dumbfounded, he remembered; the soldier looked like he was sixty.

"Really, Jackie, I've got to go -- get rolling."

"Carl, why did you come up here?" she asked in a hard voice, smoothing back her hair with one hand, her head turned to one side. She was getting sarcastic.

"To see," he said, "how you and the baby -- were getting along, I guess. I was in Milwaukee -- it wasn't that far."

He could not think of anything else to say.

"You know I don't have anybody -- to call my own," she said, stroking her hair slowly. "Stay and we can do the town."

"Ah-h," Carl said, feeling her resolve to have him stay, beginning to soften, "there must be a lot of guys around here for you to go out with --"

"Sure," she began in a high-pitched voice, "they like me for the party-girl bit, but they won't get -- serious. They don't like it -- me having the baby."

With her talking about the baby, Carl pictured himself working in an auto factory, making cars on an assembly line, walking on a concrete floor until his legs gave out. That was not for him, he thought. He was in the university to get a degree, and an office job to avoid factory work.

"We'll talk again," Carl said as they began walking again, across the farm yard. "I'm really going, now."

"You got time to meet my mother?" Jackie asked. "She's there in the kitchen."

"Next time," Carl said, knowing the excuse was weak. "I've got to roll."

They were walking up to his car, parked in the light from the kitchen windows.

"It was so nice to see you Carl -- the memories -- all came back," Jackie said, standing, her hands in the jacket pockets.

He was going to kiss her good-bye, but hesitated, feeling that part of her attraction gone.

"See you soon," Carl said, getting in the car quickly, starting the engine.

"Sure," Jackie said, looking at the car, hands in her jacket pockets, "See you soon -- soldier."

As Carl drove down the driveway in the yard, he heard a sharp <u>crack</u>, the sound a small pistol would make.

"She probably fired it, the gun Lasslett bought," Carl said, grinning. "She'll do anything -- she's desperate."

THE END

ABOUT THE AUTHOR

After college and the army service in Europe, Donald Sinclair began writing short stories from the background of his newspaper work in Detroit and Ft. Lauderdale. But it was not until his retirement in 1998 that he had the time to devote to full-time fiction book writing from the experiences he encountered. He has written five novels to date and is currently working on a sixth. Sinclair currently lives in a marina community in suburban Detroit, overlooking Lake St. Clair.